J.L. Hyde

MIDNIGHT IN DELTA COUNTY

J.L. HYDE

Midnight in Delta County

This is a work of fiction. Names, characters, places, and incidents either are the product of the author's imagination or are used fictitiously. Any resemblance to actual persons, living or dead, events, or locales is entirely coincidental.

Copyright © 2022 by J. L. Hyde

All rights reserved. No part of this book may be reproduced or used in any manner without written permission of the copyright owner except for the use of quotations in a book review.

First paperback edition October 2022

Cover Design by Allsweet Studios and Keith Kerr

Cover photo courtesy of Visit Escanaba, 2022

ISBN 979-8-9871631-0-8 (Paperback)

www.jlhyde.com

J.L. Hyde

This book is dedicated to the residents of Delta County.

Also by J. L. Hyde:

Underground

Delta County

Summer of '99

Author's Note:

Midnight in Delta County is a continuation of both Delta County and Summer of '99. If you haven't read these novels or need a refresher, please visit www.JLHyde.com for a recap.

J.L. Hyde

"Death has come to your little town, sheriff."

-Dr. Loomis
Halloween, 1978

Midnight in Delta County

Prologue

Excerpt from the best-selling book *Murder and Revenge in Delta County* by Quinn Harstead:

Voluntary manslaughter by provocation. What comes to mind when you hear those words? Self-defense, crime of passion, eye for an eye? Anywhere else in the country, a woman who was deemed mentally sane by a clinical professional after driving her car to a victim's house and strangling her on the kitchen floor would certainly be spending the majority, if not the remainder, of her life in prison. Here in Escanaba, Michigan? They take care of their own. They quietly sweep the unsavory bits right under the rug.

Mitzi Matthews, the victim in this case, wasn't on trial — but you'd never know that by listening to the witness testimony during sentencing. Mitzi's own husband took the stand in defense of his former daughter-in-law. Lisa Young, who had her vehicular manslaughter record expunged after Mitzi's actions came to light, testified via Zoom from her hospice bed shortly before her death after a courageous battle with cancer. Stifled sobs filled the courtroom as she recounted the absolute horror of learning that Mitzi was responsible for the death of her own daughter, Kelly.

Two separate witnesses received immunity for their own crimes when agreeing to testify: Tom Strenski, Delta County's Medical Examiner and Julie Prescott-Sanders, the only adult witness to the crime. Strenski detailed the mental anguish he experienced after surrendering to Mitzi's threats and a subsequent bribe of $100,000 in exchange for ruling Kelly Young's death accidental, rather than his initial determination: homicide by blunt force trauma.

Prescott-Sanders' teary-eyed admissions proved to be the most unlikely testimony of the two-day court proceedings. The mouths of spectators hung open in stunned silence as Julie avoided all eye contact while admitting she was present when Mitzi Matthews attacked Kelly Young from behind on the riverbanks behind the Buckland family camp. She confessed that she hasn't had a full night's sleep since the incident; her thoughts were permanently filled with Kelly's violent demise and Mitzi's ensuing threats to keep Julie quiet. She detailed years of manipulation and control suffered at the hands of Mitzi. Even Heather Green (who, by now, had legally dropped Matthews as her surname) gasped when she made the stunning admission that she was at Mitzi's house that fateful day to confront her about the now-infamous rocking horse. Her former mother-in-law, Cindy, let Julie in on the unspeakable cruelty behind choosing that horse as a baby shower gift, and somehow, *this* was the information that finally led to her breaking point.

She had just begun the confrontation, with shaking hands and an unsteady voice, when Heather burst through the kitchen door and attacked Mitzi. Julie also testified under oath that Mitzi had drunkenly verbalized her desire to "off" Heather on more than one occasion. When asked by Attorney Doug Angeli if she believed at any point in time that Heather's life was in danger, she quietly responded, "yes." She lived in constant fear of the woman and a single tear dribbled down her porcelain cheek as she admitted to the relief she felt when she realized she would no longer have to deal with Mitzi Matthews in her life.

Heather was stunned. She always assumed Mitzi worshipped Julie, the angelic beauty who should have married her son. She thought Julie was exempt from the consequences of Mitzi's covert narcissism, due to her family connections and ivy league education. She considered Julie to be one of the very few *worthy* of Mitzi's love and admiration. As Heather would later admit, that moment in court was the first time she sympathized with Julie. Julie, the woman who had a love child with Heather's then-husband. The woman she *certainly* never envisioned having an ounce of sympathy for.

Perhaps the most beneficial testimony was given by Heather herself. Heather Green, beloved daughter of Sally and Phil, former Miss Delta County, and adored by hundreds of thousands of social media followers around the world. You can't have a conversation with Heather and not fall a little in love with the unassuming, kind-hearted, and self-deprecating beauty. While questioned by her attorney, Doug Angeli, Heather gave calm, clear answers in such a direct manner, you never once questioned her integrity. Sitting in the back row of the courtroom, I found myself wondering what I would have done in her situation. Heather was a well-respected, law-abiding citizen who suffered several unspeakable tragedies before snapping in a moment of fury when it all became too much. Who is to say you and I wouldn't be capable of doing the same? How would you respond after finding out the same woman was responsible for the deaths of your parents *and* your best friend?

After a long beat of silence and a few seconds of shuffling papers and looking from the family section to Heather and back again, Judge Flanders announced his sentence. Heather received ten years, nine of them suspended, with credit for time served. She was also ordered to attend mandatory mental health counseling once a week for two years. Because of the extended time she spent in the Delta County Jail awaiting her day in court during the pandemic, Heather Green was free to leave the courthouse that day and finally spend unsupervised time with her infant daughter, Evelyn Kelly Green, or "Evie" for short. Assuming she doesn't violate her probation or break any laws in the next nine years, she essentially can live as a free woman.

Sighs of relief escaped the mouths of onlookers when the light sentence was handed down. I had a direct line of sight to Frank Matthews, who turned to his right and looked straight at Heather's aunt Meryl Ellison when Flanders finished his announcement. I couldn't hear everything he said, but I could easily read Frank's lips when he whispered, *"Thank God."*

PART ONE:

HEATHER

Chapter One

I crave normality. I want it more than anything I've ever wanted in my life. I had a perfectly normal existence until a killer took the lives of my parents with no warning in 2006. I was cautiously tiptoeing towards returning to a quiet life when my best friend was murdered the night of our high school reunion a decade later. For the next few years, I mistakenly thought karma was doing its job and rewarding me with a beautiful existence for all that had been tragically taken from me. I had a handsome, smart husband, a beautiful house in my hometown, and a lucrative job that didn't feel much like work at all. Soon enough, chaos found its way back into my life, and this time, it was nobody's fault but my own.

After discovering that my mother-in-law was responsible for the deaths of my parents *and* my best friend, I was confronted with the fact that my seemingly perfect husband had an affair and fathered a child with his former flame. As if this didn't already sound like the plot of a Lifetime movie, I then killed my mother-in-law in her own home and I barely remember doing it at all. All those last events took place in the course of an hour. Oh, I nearly forgot: shortly after being booked into the Delta County Jail for murder, I found out I was pregnant. If this *were* a Lifetime movie, I think I'd laugh and change the channel because it was all a little too unbelievable. Alas, it's now life as I know it.

The key to my survival has been trying my best to see the silver lining in any situation. Although I gave birth with two armed guards next to my bed, I'm now fortunate enough to be home with my beautiful, healthy daughter every night. She will have no memory of how her life started, only of the love we will give her every minute after. I had to miss the funeral of my Uncle Rick while I was incarcerated, but I was able to convince his widow, my Aunt Meryl, to move in with me when I was released. Yes, I'm still somehow living in my dream house on Ogden Avenue – just Meryl, Evie, and I. Ryan and I are officially divorced and – gasps from the crowd – he has moved in with Julie and their son. I've been out for six months, and I'm not sure how, but the co-parenting has been a lot smoother than expected. I have learned to view the man I once loved more than anything as the father of my child and nothing more. Of course, I still carry a sometimes unbearable hostility toward this man who broke my heart into a million pieces, but I've also learned that carrying anger doesn't lead to anything good in my life. As much as it hurts, I swallow it and have learned to live this life without Ryan as a partner.

In addition to the court-ordered sessions with my therapist, Vicki, we also have group counseling sessions. That's right; myself, Ryan, *and* Julie are in the same room for an hour, once every other week. I know this may seem implausible to an outsider looking in, but it has somehow begun to heal the once-irreparable damage between the three of us. Vicki's office is a safe space, and I feel at ease speaking my truth to Ryan and Julie. In the months after "the incident" (it's just much easier to say than *the homicide I committed*), Ryan was in too much shock to speak to me *or* Julie. He felt betrayed by us both. I felt betrayed by them both. It was a small, dysfunctional circle of betrayal. Julie was a not-so-innocent bystander, caught in the middle. After months of hearing the uncomfortable truths about his mother, acceptance began to set in. He has since discovered it's possible to love and miss your mother while also accepting the fact that she was a complete monster who ruined a lot of lives. Surprisingly, Mitzi's name isn't brought up much in group counseling. Vicki challenges us to work on our current situation and set attainable goals for the future, instead of focusing too much on the past. This has proven difficult for all three of us. I have despised Julie for as long as I remember and now, she is part of my life, whether I like it or not. Her statements at sentencing very well may have contributed to the leniency the judge showed me and that fact is not lost on me.

I have not seen their son since "the incident" and I don't think I'll be ready for a while. The resemblance to my husband I saw in that child's face was undeniable and constantly makes me wonder just how many people knew the truth and kept it from me.

I'm not convinced that Ryan is in love with Julie, and I realize that makes it seem like I'm in denial. I don't see any chemistry between them, and he doesn't look at her the way he used to look at me. When he holds her hand during difficult conversations in therapy, it looks obligatory. I choose to believe them when they say it was a one-time, intoxicated transgression that resulted in a pregnancy. Ryan had been annoyed by all the accusations I threw at him over the years of a secret relationship with Julie. He said the level of grief and regret he felt after that night nearly brought him to his knees. I expected this admission to offend Julie, but she agreed. I flinched when she detailed the reaction from her then-husband, Marc, when she confessed to him. I had my own experiences with Marc Sanders and knew he was a creep, but I never imagined he was capable of violence. She described how she had to wear heavy makeup for weeks to cover the bruises, and as crazy as this sounds, it comforted me to know she has Ryan around now. He may be an adulterous bastard, but he'd never hit a woman – of that, I'm certain. I'm still in contact with Marc's mother, Cindy, but I don't dare mention that during our sessions.

Something that I discuss a lot in my solo therapy appointments is the guilt I carry for the light sentence I received. I get to live my life in the free world while there are men and women incarcerated for years for far lesser crimes. Thousands of them are locked up over a drug that's now legal in most states. Vicki says it's admirable of me to be enraged over injustice when I'm the one it benefits. For most of my life, I've been disgusted by the "good old boys club" that seemingly exists in every small town. Punishment for crimes committed are directly related to your social status, that is if you even get punished at all. The very system that has disappointed me for so long in this town was the one that quietly gave me what amounts to a slap on the wrist for taking a life. Because my family was well-loved and people came out of the woodwork to describe the unspeakable acts of Mitzi Matthews, no doubt combined with the fact that Frank has connections with everyone in the court system, I received years less than I should have. I don't agree with what Vicki says – it's not admirable of me to feel guilty. Any person that receives preferential treatment in a judicial system that unfairly punishes others should feel an unbearable weight of responsibility to do something about it. I just haven't yet figured out what it is that I can do.

We are leaving a group session on an overcast Thursday in late summer when Ryan stops me in the gravel lot adjacent to the medical building that houses Vicki's office. Julie has already left in her luxury sedan to return to their McMansion on the water and wait for Dr. Ryan to return while raising their illegitimate child on recyclable packets of organic fruited nonsense. Not that I still harbor any animosity toward her.

"Yes?" I ask as he holds the driver's door of my car open and stares intently.

"We'd like to take a trip down to see Julie's aunt and uncle in Wisconsin over Labor Day weekend and bring Evie."

I nod.

"Ry, you know that's never a problem. I'll pump a little extra and freeze it. Just promise to Facetime me before bed and in the morning?"

"Great, I know I have Evie for the three-day weekend, but we'll only be gone a night or two. I don't want to spend the whole weekend away from home," he says, before lingering silently and kicking around a few small rocks with his brown dress shoes.

I squint my eyes as they meet his and shake my head slightly. I know him well enough to realize the Labor Day trip was a ploy to start a conversation so he could slip in what he'd *really* like to say.

"Heath, I'm sorry."

"For what?"

"For everything. For not being present enough. For sleeping with Julie. For ignoring all the signs that my mother was destroying you mentally. For also ignoring the signs that she was capable of…everything she did. The list goes on. I'm just sorry. I can't help but wonder how my life would look, had I made different decisions."

I give him a weak smile.

"Take it from me, if you keep wondering what life could be like, you'll drive yourself crazy. I'm just so relieved that after everything that has happened between us, we are still on speaking terms and apparently nailing this whole coparenting thing," I say.

"You're damn right we're nailing it," he replies with a smile.

A smile that unfortunately brings out that tragic dimple of his. I don't care how many years have passed or how much we've done to hurt each other; there will never be a day that dimple doesn't send a jolt through my entire body.

It's so easy to tell someone not to wonder about what might have been, but I'm finding it nearly impossible to do it myself.

Chapter Two

The end of August is in my top three favorite times of year in northern Michigan. It's still summer, so it's perfectly acceptable to walk down to the beach for an afternoon swim before coming home to drink a cold one and throw some steaks on the grill, but it's close enough to autumn that visions of pumpkins, football, crisp mornings, and falling leaves dance through my optimistic mind. I vow to slow down and appreciate this fall season more than any other in my life.

Ryan has Evie tonight and tomorrow for his off days and Meryl is in a cribbage tournament out at the casino, so I have an afternoon free of plans. This used to be something I looked forward to, but now I'm worried about being alone with my thoughts in a quiet house, so I mentally scroll through possible activities to distract me while I walk out to the mailbox at the end of my driveway. The box is nearly full, and I flip through the stack on my way back up the drive.

First, an envelope from a company I used to partner with on social media – no doubt it's a copy of the dissolution of our contract. I've received dozens of these in the last year. The only company that I hadn't heard from was the meat market here in town, but I got the Yooper version of a contract dissolution when I ran into Mr. Brown in line at the pharmacy shortly after my release and he awkwardly patted me on the back and said, "Glad yer' out kid, but how's about we back off on posting my meats to your little account for a while, eh?"

The next envelope is my water bill, which I'm dreading.

My legal fees, which is money well spent.

My therapy bill, which is money *very* well spent.

An envelope full of coupons from Elmer's County Market from Marc's mom, Cindy. She quit shopping there when her high school boyfriend took over as manager but can't bear to see the coupons go unused.

Next is People Magazine, which I'm looking forward to reading now that my small-town crime is no longer worthy of national media attention.

An envelope without a return address, with my name and address hastily scribbled in red sharpie. I don't need to open it to know it's another threatening letter, filled with bible verses, telling me what a murderous heathen I am and how I deserve to rot in hell, from a woman named Susan who very much believes she is sending these letters anonymously. She was in Mitzi's bridge club and is one of her dozen or so supporters. She's just a little more vocal than the rest. My state-of-the-art cameras caught her tiny frame putting the first few letters in my mailbox after dark before she got lazy and began letting the USPS deliver her threats across town. I don't have the patience or the desire to do anything about it, so I just toss them in the trash.

The last envelope also has a familiar look and it's without a return address, as well. I open it to find yet another cashier's check for one-thousand dollars. Just like the last six that I've received since the release of Quinn Harstead's book. I shake my head and smile. The last time I met with Quinn, she told me, "It would be illegal for you to profit off the crime you were convicted of, but if a few dollars randomly land at your doorstep, there's no way to prove where they came from."

Despite my protests, she continues to send these payments. I told her I don't *want* to profit from the death of Mitzi. I just wanted my voice to be heard and Quinn did an incredible job of making that happen. The book has been very well received. She did a fantastic job of portraying the charm of Delta County, while also giving all sides to the story so the reader can make an educated decision before passing judgment based solely on the salacious headlines. Luckily, the court of public opinion has weighed heavily in my favor. Not so lucky for Ryan, because a large number of angry women now have him listed as public enemy number one.

My phone vibrates as I'm entering my house and I smile when I see that it's the SHARK group text.

Labor Day plans? -Sam

OMG I was thinking of visiting my parents. Escanaba reunion? – Alisa

I'm in. Let's all ditch our kids and have a sleepover at Heath's. – Rebecca

I snort out a quick laugh and join the thread.

You don't have any kids, idiot. But, yes, Ryan is actually taking Evie that weekend, so bring it on. I'd love to see you guys!

After excitedly agreeing to the childless sleepover proposition, Alisa and Sam say they'll be in town next Friday around dinner time. I agree to cook for everyone at seven. Meryl is going to be overjoyed when she hears the girls are coming. She used to love sitting at the kitchen table and listening to us gossip when Kelly was still around. Meryl is everyone's favorite aunt, and in high school, we started a tradition of sleeping at her house the night before Christmas Eve. She would cook us all Swedish pancakes in the morning and listen to us dish about the cutest boys in school.

I decide to spend the rest of the afternoon planting mums outside and listening to a podcast that Alisa guest hosted this week. The episode is about moms transitioning back to the office after nearly two years of working from home, and she has a lot to say on the subject. I smile as I put my headphones in, and press play to hear Alisa's sweet yet confident voice socking it to the corporate patriarchy.

Normally I like to garden without my headphones in so I can listen to the birds and other sounds from Ludington Park, but since my release, they've become a necessity. Most people who walk by won't enter my yard and speak to me directly, but I can hear them not-so-discreetly wondering if I'm *that* Heather Matthews as they slow their pace in front of the house. Hearing their half-ass attempts at whispering slander is somehow worse than if they approached me directly, so I just plug my ears and listen to yacht rock or whichever podcast has caught my attention that week. I also used to love sitting on the rocking chairs on my front porch, but now any leisurely outdoor time is spent in the backyard, behind the privacy of my six-foot fence.

I'm carefully placing a group of mums into the soil of a large planter and listening to Alisa describe the benefits of a home-office hybrid schedule when a hand is placed gently on my shoulder, yet still manages to momentarily make my heart stop. I fall over from my crouched position and land squarely on my ass, while simultaneously pulling the headphones from my ears.

"Frank!"

He has his right hand up in defense, his left hand gripping a brown paper bag with Applewood Eatery stamped on the front, which he thrusts forward to show me.

"I'm sorry, I tried to get your attention when I parked, but you didn't hear me. I brought you lunch," he says with an apologetic shrug.

"Oh, Frank. You're so wonderful. I could use a break, and I'm starving. Let's go inside."

"That sounds like a plan, kid," he responds.

I see him glance to the right of the front door as we enter. There is a patio seating arrangement opposite the rocking chairs, that features an incredibly comfortable padded sectional with a coffee table in front. He raises his hand to suggest it, looks into my eyes, and quickly grasps why I don't want to dine outside, exposed. It's a shame; the weather is perfect for it today.

As I'm washing my hands in the kitchen, Frank begins unpacking the contents of the bag and I note there are three sandwiches and three bags of chips. He's not-so-casually looking around the house as he sets them out on the breakfast table.

"Meryl is at a cribbage tournament out at the casino, but I bet she'll be starving when she gets home. How about I put it in the fridge for her?" I ask, trying to suppress my grin. "Oh, chicken salad, her favorite."

"Oh, is it?" he asks, feigning ignorance.

"Sure is," I respond with a smile.

Lisa, who was undeniably the love of Frank's life, has been gone for a little over a year. So has Meryl's husband, Rick. There was a little mutual infatuation between the two in high school, over forty years ago, but Meryl never acted on it because of concern over their different social statuses. He has been dropping by out of the blue the last few months, under the guise of checking on me, but he always manages to focus his attention solely on Meryl when she's here. She's a little oblivious to his advances, so I'm just letting it play out without getting involved. God knows I need the entertainment around here.

"You know, Frank, I just logged into my bank account, and I see you still haven't cashed my rent checks."

He unwraps his sandwich and shrugs his shoulders as he takes a bite.

"It's your house, my dear. You shouldn't be writing rent checks."

I pull open my bag of chips and smile when I see they are dill pickle, my favorite.

"And you loaned us the money for the house, which means I still need to pay you back. I've been picking up more hours at the bookstore and I can afford it, I promise," I say. I don't mention that I'm also receiving unsolicited checks from the woman who wrote a best-selling book about his wife's demise.

"We can revisit the topic next summer, how's that?"

I shake my head.

"Oh, Frank. I'm certain I don't deserve all that you continue to do for me. Thank you."

He puts his hand over mine, which was just about to pick up half of my sandwich.

"Kid, you've been through the wringer, and some of it may have even been my fault. It's the least I can do."

"We both have, Frank."

We finish the rest of our meals, mostly in silence. Whether I'm alone or in the presence of someone involved in *the incident*, the silence is always the worst. My thoughts race through the possible options of what could be going through his head. *Does he regret supporting me after what I did? Is he happy that Ryan and Julie are together? Is he thinking of Lisa?*

"I was just thinking about some nice big pots I saw on sale at Menards. If you hold off on planting the last two mums, I'll pick them up for you. They'd look great on each side of the garage."

I laugh.

"What?"

"Nothing, Frank. That sounds wonderful. Thank you for thinking of me."

Chapter Three

Later, I'm sitting on the couch and lacing up my walking shoes when Meryl comes through the garage door just before midnight.

"Okay, night owl! Tell me you at least won a few bucks!" I laugh.

"Oh, Heath, I smoked em' all. I got a twenty-eight hand around ten o'clock and that miserable Sandy McCarthy got so disgusted with my luck, she walked out!" she says, throwing her worn-out leather purse on the kitchen counter and collapsing in one of the reading chairs by the window. "I haven't had a twenty-eight in years. What a night."

It's so nice to see her smiling again. After Rick passed, she lost the light in her eyes for a while, understandably. She put on a brave face for our visits, but I could tell she was letting grief get the best of her. It killed me that I was behind bars instead of consoling her, all because of my actions.

"Frank brought us sandwiches today, I put yours in the fridge," I say, raising my eyebrows a few times.

"I'm starving. What a guy," she declares as she hops back on her feet and heads to the fridge. I'm not sure where this woman gets her energy, but after twelve hours at the casino, I'd be struggling to keep my eyes open. She unwraps the sandwich to see it's her favorite and shrugs so nonchalantly, I nearly choke on my laugh. *These two, I swear.*

"Alright, well, Ryan has Evie tonight, so I'm headed out for a little stroll."

I prepare for what I'm sure is coming next. The same thing she says every time I walk after dark.

"Oh, Heath, it's nearly midnight. I sure wish you wouldn't walk alone."

"Oh, are you going to come with me?" I ask, knowing damn well she isn't.

"Well, no, but it sure would make me feel better if you took the pepper spray I keep in my purse. And promise me you'll keep your phone on you the whole time," she says as she reaches into her bag and hands me a pink pepper spray can, adorned with cheap, clear jewels and an "M" engraved on the side. "Your Uncle Rick gave me this after we started having car break-ins on our block. I've never used it, so it's got plenty of juice left."

I put the canister in the pocket of my joggers. *Plenty of juice left.* I smile.

"Alright, Mer. Now I feel well-equipped to fight off the midnight street thugs of Escanaba, Michigan. I'll be back in about an hour," I half-shout on my way out the door, not giving her the chance to argue any further.

I pause on the front porch and take a deep breath. Fall is coming. The midnight hour has become my own little slice of serenity. There are no onlookers getting whiplash as I walk by, no hushed commentary as I politely smile and wave, and no discreet cell phone videos being taken. Just me and this cold, dark, northern night.

I turn right and head toward Ludington Park; the only sounds in the night are my shoes hitting the pavement and crickets chirping merrily in every direction. As I cross Lake Shore Drive and near the beach, the lapping of waves invites me off my usual route and down the narrow, sandy path to the water. The moon is enormous tonight and casts a haunting glow over the trees. I find a spot and collapse slowly, my hands landing in the cool, soft mounds of sand. My fingers swim through it, picking up handfuls at a time and slowly letting the grains escape my grip. I close my eyes and listen to the waves for what seems like an hour. I don't remember the last time I felt at peace like this. For a brief moment, my troubles floated away, over the soothing waves of Lake Michigan.

I wish everyone could escape like this. These night walks have become the catalyst for my greatest ideas, solutions to life's most troubling problems, and answers to the questions that nag my every waking thought. It's tonight, under this perfect Sturgeon Moon, that I decide to take the necessary actions and regain control of my life – the life I want.

I will live in a way that sets an example for Evie and honors the memory of my parents. I will atone for my sins. I will be good and honest every day of my life. I will tell the people around me that I love them any chance I get.

I will lead an existence so uneventful; you'd be bored to tears just hearing about it. If I want a quiet, normal life, I'm just going to have to be the captain of my ship and create it myself.

Chapter Four

"And if she fusses, remember the pink blanket with the elephant tends to soothe her. She's been randomly waking up once around three, but really falls back asleep quickly. Oh, and the dishwasher sounds on Spotify will knock her right out in the car, and –"

"Heather!" Ryan shouts with a smile, putting his arm on my shoulder. "You do remember that I'm her father, and I have had her a minimum of two nights a week since the day she was born. It's me, Ryan Matthews."

Why was I so casual when I agreed to let Ryan and Julie take her this weekend? He caught me with my guard down. I was carefree and soothed by Vicki's encouraging advice after a particularly successful session. Maybe I should reconsider. I could cancel the SHARKs tonight and just stay home all weekend with Evie.

"Don't you dare change your mind. We are so excited to have the weekend with her. And I heard the girls are coming to town, so give yourself a break and have some fun," he pleads, reading my mind.

He's wearing khakis and a Vineyard Vines crewneck sweatshirt, which is about as casual as Ryan can get. I can tell he's really looking forward to the long weekend, so I swallow my hesitation and hand Evie to him. Her tiny hands go directly to his cheeks, and she giggles as he kisses her nose. I remind myself that I'm simply enamored with Ryan as a father, not as a partner. I must repeat that every time he picks her up for his custody days. He can be an excellent father and also a horrible, adulterous husband.

I carry her diaper bag and open the front door so Ryan and Evie can pass through. His vehicle is parked in the driveway, and it still gives me a shot to the heart each time I see Julie sitting in the passenger seat. The seat that once belonged to me. I wave my hand and give her a cordial smile as we approach the SUV. I stop when I see a second car seat in the back. I'm not sure why it's only occurring to me now that *their* son, Hunter, will also be on the trip.

"Well, here's her bag. You guys have a safe trip and please shoot me a text when you get there," I say, angling my body away from the vehicle.

Ryan's eyebrows furrow momentarily before he registers the reason for my hesitation.

I force a smile, give Evie five quick kisses all over her face, and wave goodbye as he holds her up and makes airplane noises to distract her, before "flying" her into her car seat. I resist the urge to double-check the straps before he closes the door. He's her father. He's a doctor. He's fully capable of making sure she's securely fastened. Deep breaths, Heather. Deep breaths.

After a long nap, shower, and cry, I'm on the back deck with Meryl and lighting the grill in anticipation of the SHARK's arrival. I finally pop open a can of beer with relief when Ryan texts to let me know they've made it to Julie's family's house. He sends me a picture of her aunt and uncle holding Evie and they look overjoyed. I set my disdain for Julie aside and feel gratitude that my daughter has an extended family to love her. Julie's relatives have zero obligation to welcome Evie into their lives, yet they all have, with enthusiastic, open arms. For that, I'm thankful.

"Well, it's Labor Day weekend, I guess I might as well have one, too," Meryl says innocently as she reaches into the cooler and pops open a Busch Light.

"Mer, that's like your third. Who do you think you're fooling?" I laugh and snap my tongs a few times in her direction.

She huffs.

"Sorry, officer, I didn't know you were the beer-countin' police," she shakes her head and slides the can into her faded yellow Green Bay Packers koozie.

We hear a car pull in the driveway a few minutes later and judging by the time (fifteen minutes early), I assume it's Alisa. My suspicions are confirmed as she slides the patio door open with her foot, her arms holding an oversized charcuterie board.

"I told you not to bring anything," I say, squinting my eyes and giving her a few disapproving snaps of my tongs, as well.

"It's just a little something I threw together," she responds, setting the board on the patio table and leaning forward to hug Meryl. "I think of you all the time. How *are* you?" she asks. Alisa has a way of making every person she speaks to believe that they are the center of the universe. She exists solely to listen to your problems, hear your thoughts, and cater to your every need. It must be exhausting.

Meryl places both of her hands over Alisa's. "Don't tell the others, but you've always been my favorite."

I roll my eyes accordingly and give Alisa a quick hug before escaping into the kitchen to grab the chicken thighs that have been marinating all day. Just as I pull the tray out of the fridge, my front door swings open. Sam and Rebecca come plowing through with an oversized Yeti cooler and an Elmer's grocery bag.

"What is it with you jerks? I told you not to bring anything!" I say with a laugh.

"We don't have to see our kids for twenty-four hours; I think you're grossly underestimating how much we are going to drink, Heath," says Sam.

Rebecca sets the brown paper grocery bag on the counter and hugs me, nearly making me drop my tray of chicken. She pulls back, places both of her hands on the sides of my face, and stares at me with concern.

"Heath, you are all skin and bones. Are you eating?" she asks.

"Well, I'm trying to eat these chicken thighs, but you're in my way," I respond with a cocky smile and a wink. "Grab the pasta salad out of the fridge for me and get your asses outside."

It's true; I haven't been taking the best care of myself. After my epiphany at the beach the other night, I vowed to change that. I need to make my health a top priority. Evie and Meryl depend on me, and I'm doing them no favors if I'm not feeling my best.

For the next hour or so, my mind slowly drifts into a deceiving, euphoric place where life feels so good, I could cry. I didn't lose my family, I didn't commit a crime that landed me in jail for over a year, and on the cover of every magazine in America, and I didn't become notorious overnight. Tonight, on this beautiful Friday evening, I'm sitting on the patio with my best friends and my favorite aunt, and all is well in my soul. I've drank three beers, which is just enough to see everything around me in blissful, rose-colored glasses, but not enough to lose my inhibitions or spend the night on the bathroom tile. This in-between is a hard high to chase, but I've caught it tonight.

As I'm clearing everyone's plates, I hear a honk out front and nearly drop the stack from my arms.

"Ahh, that's Paula. Gotta go," Meryl half-shouts as she slips her shoes on and dashes into the house to grab her purse.

"Mer, it's nearly bedtime. Where in the hell are you going with Paula?" I ask.

"Headed out west. Player's Club points get loaded to our cards at midnight tonight and they are doing a holiday weekend bonus. See ya, kid."

Out west. *The casino.* Fourteen miles west of Escanaba.

"Don't wait up!" she shouts as she slams the front door behind her.

I set the dishes down in the sink and turn back to face my friends. They all seem entertained by Meryl's love for gambling, which I'm fairly sure borders on addiction, but that's a discussion for another day.

"I love Mer so much, it hurts," says Rebecca.

"We'll see how much you love her when you're fast asleep tonight and she comes banging in at 3 a.m. making herself a ham sandwich, which she insists on microwaving to *take the chill off* for some insane reason," I counter.

As I sit back down with the girls, there's a small relief that Mer has left the party. It's been a while since the four of us sat around and talked without interruptions or distractions. Per usual, Alisa starts with uncomfortable questions.

"Heath…so, how *are* you doing? Don't lie to us. You can tell us anything."

The sun has fully set, and my string lights have clicked on, illuminating the backyard with a dreamy yellow glow. Rebecca and Sam are holding their breath, awaiting my response. The only person who knows *exactly* how I'm doing is Vicki, my therapist. I shield everyone else in my life from the hard truths because it's a lot to carry. It's easier for those around me to think I'm handling everything swimmingly, so their burden of friendship is just a little lighter. I've been doing this my whole life.

"Some days are hard; most days are just fine," I answer, which is mostly the truth. "The more time passes, the hard days get fewer and fewer," I add, which is mostly a lie.

"Do you think you and Ryan will ever get back together?" Sam asks. Rebecca slaps her arm. "What, it's a valid question!" Sam retorts.

"It is a valid question. The only Heather anyone knows is the Heather that's tied to Ryan. It's been a weird transition to just Heather," I say, and Alisa rubs my back in encouragement.

"To answer your question, no. Too much has happened. We've hurt each other worse than I thought possible, and I think in the last few months we've formed a great relationship as co-parents. I can't imagine a life where a romantic relationship could exist again between us. He's with Julie now. And I'm okay with that. Not to mention, if I gave him another chance, I think there would be a hundred women on my front lawn with pitchforks."

"We just want you to be happy," says Rebecca. "Not just because we hate Julie."

I laugh. "I know that Becs. One day I won't be known as the *Mother-in-Law Murderer*, and maybe life will start to look normal again."

Alisa sits a little straighter and turns to me.

"May I remind you that, although the tabloids gave you that God-awful name, nearly every person in America sympathized with you? I've never seen a convicted murderer receive support as you did. You make my job easy."

I smile and remind Alisa that I'm not her client. Her self-launched PR campaign on my behalf has been completely out of my control and undeniably without my approval.

"Speaking of public support, any plans to return to social media?" she asks.

"The thought of reactivating that account gives me hives. Ask me again in a few months."

This seems to pacify her, and she concludes her interrogation.

The conversation thankfully shifts to which movie we're going to watch before bed when my phone lights up. It's face up on the patio table and I can see from the signature blue logo that it's an alert from my security system. This time of night, it's normally a chipmunk or a neighborhood cat scampering by the motion-detecting cameras. I lean forward to retrieve it and swipe to view the alert.

My heart stops when I review the footage that set off the sensor. I zoom in and see red. It's everywhere; my driveway, my garage door, my lawn. Bright, crimson, splattered blood red.

Chapter Five

Alisa hears me gasp and looks over my shoulder.

"What the hell?" she whispers, and the other two girls join her.

"Who the hell is that?" asks Rebecca.

I zoom in to study the petite figure in black. The person is standing so close to my garage door; I can only see them from behind. Their right arm is raised, and I spot what appears to be a paintbrush in their grip and a bucket at their feet. I scan up and see the letters "M", "U", and "R" painted sloppily across the white garage doors.

"Susan damned Grant is who it is," I mutter.

"The little lady from the flower shop?" Alisa asks.

"The little lady from the flower shop, who is also one of Mitzi's very vocal supporters. She's been on a harassment campaign since I got released."

"Should we call the cops?" asks Sam.

"Nah, I'm not interested in having my name in the paper ever again. Let her get out her frustration. I can repaint the door."

"Let's have a little fun, Heath," Sam says with a twinkle in her eyes, reminiscent of her excitement when coming up with countless diabolical plans in high school.

"I could use some fun," Alisa agrees.

Within minutes, we have gone upstairs and climbed out of my master bedroom window, onto the slanted dormer that connects to the highest peak of the roof. I can't help but hear my mother's disapproving voice as four slightly intoxicated women climb a roof in the pitch black of night with no safety precautions whatsoever. No matter how much time passes, that voice never quite does go away.

We creep quietly but swiftly over the peak of the roof and scoot down to the top of the garage. We line up in a row and peek over the edge to see Susan nearly finished with her "MURDERER" graffiti masterpiece. Unless she decides to include a bible verse below it, as she often does in her letters, our time is running out.

We are all on our knees, leaning over the edge with our hands filled with the haphazardly gathered supplies for our quickly organized mission. We each look left and right and nod to confirm our plan.

"Now," Sam whispers, and total chaos rains right over poor Susan.

Sam and Rebecca have pitchers of water, Alisa has a bag of phallic-shaped confetti left over from a friend's bachelorette party, and I have a bag of flour, which is now ripped open and emptied over Susan's head. For a moment, she is stunned. She let out a brief yelp when the first pitcher of water dumped over her head, knocking the black bandana down off her nose, and exposing her face. She looks straight up at us, her entire face and head covered in wet, clumped bits of flour and multi-colored glittered confetti, formed in X-rated shapes that might just get her kicked out of the Christian ladies' bridge club. Alisa snaps a picture with her flash on and yells "Leave our friend alone or this picture is getting circulated all over Saint Patrick's church this Sunday, SUSAN!"

Susan gasps, coughs out a few pieces of confetti, drops her supplies, and runs. We all laugh when we see she has only parked a block away and we can clearly see her Chrysler minivan with an obnoxious bumper sticker that reads *"It's a GRANT thing, you wouldn't understand."* Alisa snaps another picture of her getting in the driver's side for good measure. We all collapse on our backs and laugh for an eternity. I needed this. I needed this so, so badly.

"Let's go clean up her mess," says Sam, who begins crawling over the peak, back to my bedroom window.

"No, guys, I've got this. It's my problem. I can't thank you enough for everything you've already done," I say. "I've got some extra white paint in the garage if I can't wash it off with soap and water."

"I texted Mitch so you can claim it on your homeowner's insurance and pay someone else to do the work," says Alisa, holding up her phone and wearing a smug grin of satisfaction.

"Alisa! It's the middle of the night. Leave that poor man alone. I'll just clean it up. We'd probably have to file a police report to claim it anyway, and I'm not doing that."

Her phone dings and she quickly reads the text. She smiles and turns the screen around toward me.

Don't clean it yet. This I've gotta see. OMW.

"My personal property was destroyed by a very small, but angry, bridge-playing spitfire of a woman; this doesn't need to be entertainment for the entire town!" I snap.

This makes them all keel over in a fit of laughter.

"I'm glad he's coming, I miss our sweet Mitchell," says Alisa.

"Yeah, yeah," I mutter, hoisting myself into my bedroom window like a teenager. "Me, too."

Mitch walks up Ogden Avenue before I finish filling my bucket with soap and water. He's clapping as he approaches us in front of the garage with a smile so big, I can't help but smile a little myself.

"Damn, Heath, you've got this little old lady worked up!"

I shake my head.

"I curse the day you moved to the south side," I mutter, reaching down to submerge my oversized sponge in the bucket.

"I didn't know you moved," says Sam, moving closer to give Mitch a quick hug.

"Two blocks away. Somebody has to keep an eye on Green," he responds, jutting his chin toward me.

"Well, keep a closer eye. Susan Grant has been harassing her for months," snaps Alisa.

Mitch furrows his brow and takes a few steps in my direction.

"Is that true, Heath? Why aren't we getting the police involved?"

I take my first swipe at the red paint and exhale when I see that it's easily fading away. I'll scrub off the rest with the sponge, hit it with the hose, and it will be good as new. It will take the light of day to hose off what she spilled in the driveway and lawn, but I'll have the time tomorrow.

I drop the sponge back into the bucket and put my hands on my hips.

"First of all, I hope I never see another police officer as long as I live. Second, everyone grieves differently. Susan's way of grieving her friend is to be rightfully angry at the person who took her away. Let's give it some time."

Sam lets out a short laugh. "You're a better person than me, Heather Green."

"Well, I'm not perfect. I was just about to remind Alisa to send me those incriminating pictures of Susan so I can look at them when I'm feeling low," I say.

"I've already sent them to the group text. And Mitch," she smiles.

Mitch takes his phone out of his back pocket and swipes it open, briefly studying the picture before shaking his head and putting it back.

"You SHARKs are something else. Always have been."

"Always will be," Alisa responds with a wink.

Chapter Six

I wake up to a text from Quinn Harstead. After another beer or two, I sent her the pictures of Susan Grant with a clown emoji, well into the early hours of the morning. Quinn has received a few emails from Susan, letting her know exactly what she thinks about her book and reminding her that she has a special reservation in hell for giving me a voice. Quinn also knows about the letters I've been getting. Until last night, she's the only one who knew.

Literally, day made. You guys are legends. Maybe she'll leave us both alone now? -Q

It's still surreal to consider Quinn Harstead a person that I can text at any hour. Other than Kevin Chown, a bass player that has been touring with the world's most famous musicians for decades, Quinn is the only "celebrity" from Delta County. My notoriety doesn't exactly gain me entry to their club, yet they've both become what I'd consider to be my friends in recent years.

I genuinely hope she's right and Susan will move on. I understand her anger, but showing up at my house in the middle of the night is crossing all sorts of lines. Thank goodness Frank had those security cameras installed for me. The thought of a faceless vandal outside my home is infinitely more terrifying than knowing for certain it was Susan Grant.

The girls and I spend the lazy Saturday afternoon eating Swedish pancakes and napping off our hangovers in the late summer sun on my back patio.

I'm deep in the middle of a dream about being chased by Mitzi through a tight tunnel in some sort of underground cave when Meryl startles me awake and I nearly flip over in my hammock. Once I gain my bearings, I giggle at how rough she looks. The only color on her splotchy, pale face is the blue under her eyes and her matted hair looks like it hasn't been combed in a week.

"Mer," I whisper. "What time did you get back?"

"I don't want to talk about it, kid. Just tell me where you hid the Extra Strength Tylenol."

"My bathroom, middle drawer. You might also want to grab my eye mask out of the fridge; it does wonders for headaches."

She pats my arm softly.

"Thanks, Heath. I went outside to grab the paper and there was a bunch of glittered penises scattered across the driveway and red paint splatters everywhere. For a minute, I thought it was blood. You kids have a crazy night or what?"

I snort.

"I'll tell you all about it later. Go get some rest."

I scan the backyard and see Sam and Alisa soundly asleep on the outdoor sectional and Rebecca snoring steadily on the other hammock. A memory floats through my mind of a similar scene from our junior year of high school. The SHARKs, when Kelly was still here, decided that we would attempt to stay up all night watching scary movies. We made it until around six in the morning when we passed out one by one in my basement family room during the opening credits of *The Lost Boys*. My dad wanted to surprise us with a dozen jelly-filled from The Donut Connection, but quietly tiptoed back upstairs when he found us fast asleep. When we groggily strolled up to the kitchen around noon, he was waiting at the breakfast table, anxious to hear all about our movie marathon and give us the donuts. I remember thinking he was so lame and embarrassing for waiting on us to wake up and being entirely too excited about donuts, but now the vision makes me choke back tears. He loved me so much. He just wanted to spend time with me and my friends and hear about the things that interested us, like horror movies. I promise to make Evie feel that loved every day of her life, even if it does embarrass her in front of her friends.

Shortly before dinnertime, Sam and Alisa pack up their bags and prepare to head back to their parents' houses to their children and husbands.

"Suckers," Rebecca mumbles as they go over the kids' daycare and back-to-school schedules for the following week.

"You're just jealous because we both get to work 50-hour work weeks and give half our paychecks to daycares that send our children home with a new virus every month," jokes Sam. I'm so fortunate that Meryl watches Evie on the days I work at the bookstore. I can't imagine trusting strangers to take care of her, let alone ones that are stretched thin and watching dozens of other kids at the same time. I don't dare mention this to Alisa and Sam, who have no choice in the matter.

"I see your daycare viruses and raise you…working at a hospital full time during a pandemic," Rebecca responds with both hands palms up and a shrug.

"Touché," they both say in unison.

"What are you going to do for the rest of your childless weekend?" Sam asks me.

I hadn't really thought about it until now.

"Probably nurse Mer back to health, catch up on Netflix, and stop at the bookstore tomorrow to unpack the new arrivals."

Alisa shrugs her duffle bag strap over her shoulder and grabs her car keys from the counter.

"You know, if you reactivated your social media accounts, you wouldn't have to work at the bookstore. I bet you have dozens of companies wanting to do sponsored deals," she says.

"It's not a high-powered career in PR, Alisa, but I actually enjoy it. Now get out of here so I can watch *Working Moms*. I'm two seasons behind."

A few hours later, I successfully finished five episodes, served a still-hungover Mer an early dinner on a tray in her room, finished two loads of laundry, and somehow ended up crashing in the rocking chair up in Evie's quiet nursery.

This room is everything I dreamed it would be when we bought the house. With its pale-green walls and assortment of light-yellow jungle animals dancing across the wallpaper, it was created with a unisex vibe in case Ryan and I decided to have more children. Let's all laugh at the absurdity of how that plan sounds now.

When Evie is here, I'm constantly picking up toys, stocking diapers, hanging up her little outfits in the closet, and stopping her from crawling out of the room. Now that she's gone for the weekend, the silence is nearly unbearable. There are days when she's acting particularly feisty and combative, and I dream of an afternoon of silence and zero responsibilities. Now that she's gone, I'd give anything to hear her tiny little voice throwing a fit.

My self-pity party is interrupted by my cell phone vibrating in my hand — I didn't realize I was even holding it.

It's Frank.

There's a mass dedicated to Lisa and Kelly tomorrow at 8 a.m. at a local Catholic church. He'd like me to join him. He knows that I haven't attended mass since my parents died in 2006. My first instinct is, of course, to decline. Before I send the text, I erase it and tell him I'll see him there. I can feel his excitement through the phone when he responds with his immense appreciation that I've agreed to come. This man has done more for me in the last two years than I can even wrap my head around; the least I can do is attend a one-hour mass in honor of two women we both loved very much.

The sun is beginning to set, and I decide to put my walking shoes on and do something I haven't been able to do in a long time: sit on my front porch for a while. The commitment to attend tomorrow's mass has given me a renewed determination to reintroduce myself to the community again. I miss the parks, I miss the beach on a sunny day, I miss the restaurants. I'm going to sit on my front porch, in my favorite rocking chair, for the next few hours before I take my walk. If people gawk; let them. I'll wave. If people whisper, I'll whisper back. Maybe Alisa is right, and the animosity is all in my head. Maybe the public isn't nearly as angry with me as I tell myself.

When I jog down the wooden steps to the main level of the house, Meryl is on the couch, socked feet kicked up on the ottoman and a bloody mary in her hand. She's still looking tired, but infinitely better than she did this morning. *You've Got Mail* is playing on the TV; it's her comfort movie.

"Getting back on the horse that bucked 'ya?" I ask with a smile, raising my eyebrows.

"Where the hell are you going this early?" she asks, ignoring my dig about her drink. "It's not nearly midnight."

"Well, Mer, I'm going to go sit out on my beautiful front porch for a while and watch the world go by," I say with pride.

"Well, la-ti-da," she mumbles, unimpressed while taking a sip of her drink.

Maybe this isn't as big of a milestone as I'd thought. I ignore her lack of enthusiasm, grab a Sprite Zero from the fridge, and head out the front door. I can do this. It's my front porch. If people walking by have a problem, it has nothing to do with me. I'm a free woman, just living her life. I envy the fact that Ryan so easily leaves the house, casually deflecting the insults thrown his way.

I take a seat on the rocking chair and exhale. This is it. This is the life I dreamed of when we bought the house. Well, the dream scenario included Ryan in the other rocking chair, but it's still pretty nice. I can hear a band playing in the park and the sounds of delighted people enjoying the holiday weekend. I hold my breath when a group of teenage girls walks by, but they don't even look at me. After a few moments, I grow restless. Why can't I just rock on this chair and enjoy the silence like my grandma used to do for hours? She was a waitress at the local pizza place for over thirty years, and once her kids were grown and her husband passed, her nights were spent on the porch with a brandy slush and not a care in the world.

Maybe I should grab a book.

I dash inside and down the stairs to what used to be Ryan's office and is now my reading room. Quinn Harstead's latest novel is sitting on my end table, a bookmark placed between the first and second chapters. It's not that the book isn't interesting; I just haven't had the attention span to sit down and focus on reading in a while.

Although she began her career writing novels, she's mostly known for her factual true-crime books. Apparently, this one is quite dark and a departure from her normal writing style, but it was an instant hit. It stayed on the New York Times Bestsellers list for eight consecutive weeks. It takes place in Delta County, leading a lot of readers to mistake it for non-fiction, despite her bold disclaimer at the beginning of the book. Meryl told me that she overheard two ladies at her hair salon talking about how Quinn made a million dollars in three months from this book alone. I highly doubt that, but she's doing just fine for herself. I grab the book and head back outside.

As I'm sitting back down on the porch, an older couple passes by. They are walking hand in hand away from the park. I also notice the music has stopped; the Labor Day festivities must be concluding. I once again hold my breath as they notice me, but they both just smile and wave politely, with not a single hint of recognition in their eyes. Over the next hour, dozens more pass by without a whisper, dirty look, or otherwise disrespectful gesture. Maybe this all is blowing over and I can begin to quietly soft step back into normalcy.

"Heather Green!" someone shouts from my left and I nearly choke on my drink as I plan my escape. I spoke too soon; I can't sit out here unnoticed. I knew it.

The relief in my body when I turn my head to see that it's Mitch walking up the concrete path to my porch is unreal. I wipe the Sprite from the front of my shirt and set my book down at my feet while I stand to greet him.

"I can't tell you how happy I am to see you," I tell him.

"Wow, have you been drinking, Ms. Green?"

I smile.

"No, I'm just trying to get comfortable sitting out front again. I haven't done it since my release."

His smile fades and he jogs up the steps and takes a seat next to me, leaning forward and putting both his hands on my knees as I also take a seat.

"I'm so sorry, Heath. I didn't even realize you hadn't been sitting out here. I can't imagine what it's like to live in such a small community after everything that's happened. Have you considered moving?"

Yes, of course, I've considered moving. If it weren't for Evie, I'd probably be halfway to Mexico by now.

"Everyone that Evie loves is here. Hell, the few of you left who love *me* are all here. It just wouldn't make sense to leave."

"Well, I can't say I'm upset by that. I hope you stay forever," he slaps my knee before sitting back in his chair. "I can't wait until Evie's old enough for me to teach her about football. She's going to be cheering for the green and gold before she starts kindergarten; that's a promise."

I roll my eyes.

"Go have your own kid, Miller."

He looks past me at the book sitting on the ground and subtly shakes his head.

"What? You don't like Quinn Harstead?" I ask.

"Well, her last book included an entire chapter portraying me as a suspect in Kelly Young's murder, so I'm not exactly the president of her fan club."

"May I remind you that I'm the one who initially considered you a suspect? She was just doing her job by accurately depicting *everyone* who could have done it. Chapter eight suggests Ryan and I were capable, remember?"

"Yeah, yeah. I just think she lost touch with what it's like to be a member of this community when she started making millions. She's been living in that mansion in the woods too long."

I slap his arm.

"Hey now, I consider Quinn a friend. Maybe you should meet her and give her a chance. She's quite lovely. You and her husband would hit it off, I just know it."

This time, he rolls his eyes.

"Where are you coming from, anyway?" I ask.

He hesitates for a minute, before fighting back a smile.

"Mitch Miller! Were you on a date?"

He throws his head back and laughs loudly.

"God, no. I was just down in the park getting Norm's fries, and I didn't want to tell you because I ate them all on the way up here. I'm sorry, I know they are your favorite."

I hop out of my chair and put him in a playful headlock.

"You bastard!"

We spend the next hour talking about everything and nothing at all as the sounds from the park completely fade out. It's nearly midnight, and everyone has gone home to sleep off a day of consuming cheap beer, that probably began at the parade on Ludington Street twelve hours ago. Yoopers do not play around when it comes to day drinking at holiday festivals. The beer tent on the 4th of July regularly raises enough proceeds to fund local charities for an entire year.

As Mitch stands to leave, he asks me for the third time if I'm *sure* I want to walk alone this late at night. I reassure him, also for the third time, that I do this regularly and have never encountered anything to be worried about. I also pull Mer's pepper spray out of my pocket and his eyes crinkle at the edges when he sees the bedazzled canister. He hugs me goodbye, and I may be imagining it, but the embrace lasts a little longer than usual. Maybe he is really worried about me.

I start my normal path down to Lake Shore Drive and inhale the burnt remnants of smoke from store-bought firecrackers, veering off into the grass of neighboring homes several times to avoid the debris on the sidewalk. It may sound funny coming from someone convicted of manslaughter, but nothing enrages me like littering. It's just so damn disrespectful. Maybe I'll take a walk back down here before mass in the morning with a trash bag and some gloves; it's the least I can do to begin to make amends with this community.

Against my will, thoughts of Mitch keep popping into my mind. I haven't thought about a man romantically in as long as I can remember.

Between jail cells and court dates, my survival and the life of my child have taken all mental priority. As much as I hate to admit it, picturing Mitch on the front lawn with Evie, teaching her to play catch, makes me swoon. When he hugged me on the porch, a tingling sensation shot up my body that I haven't felt in years. I've known Mitch since we were kids and not once have I thought of him as anything other than a friend. Okay, or briefly, a suspect in Kelly's murder. I'm probably just tired, lonely, and not thinking straight.

I decide to take a right on Lake Shore and loop down Loren W. Jenkins Memorial Drive, which takes me by the tennis courts and playground before continuing to the marina and Sand Point Lighthouse. I read somewhere that changing up something as small as your walking routine or your drive to work can keep you mentally sharp. It's never too early to think about preventing Alzheimer's, or at least that's what Rebecca always tells me.

As I pass by the courts, I decide to try my hand at jogging. I've never been much of an athlete, but I know it would burn more calories and get my heart rate up – this bit of advice coming from Alisa. I take off, and the first minute is spent telling myself how easy this is and how maybe I *am* meant to be a jogger. I'm young enough to take up a new hobby; I can do this every night. By the time I make it to the four-way intersection a half mile ahead, I'm tempted to take a right and collapse on the sand beach. Turns out, as initially suspected, I am *not* a jogger.

I stay straight, toward the marina, and I'm still struggling to catch my breath as I approach the boat slips, both hands bracing my lower back, which is now throbbing. It's a quiet night, which amplifies the sound of gentle waves lapping on the sides of the boats. I've lived by water most of my life, and somehow, have never been on a sailboat. Maybe *that* can be my next hobby to conquer. Reluctantly, I think about how much my social media following would enjoy having a front-row seat to my boating misadventures. I'm not sure if I'll ever log back in, but I sure do miss it some days.

As I near the lighthouse, I smile at the memory of how much it terrified me as a child. A large plaque outside details the history, including the eerie description of the mysterious fire that killed the lighthouse keeper, Mary Terry, in 1886. That was nightmare fuel for a gangly group of 6th graders during the first summer our parents let us bike down to the marina unsupervised. I've even toured it as an adult, and it still sent chills up my spine. I'm not sure the rumors are true of her spirit haunting the place, but let's just say it's not a building I want to spend time in alone at midnight. As I near the structure, I pick up my pace at the thought.

Something catches my eye as I'm passing by and my heart skips a beat when I realize it's a person, sitting on the ground, leaning up against the white wooden door of the lighthouse. They are staring straight at me. The gate to the fence that surrounds the property is locked each night when they close. I briefly wonder if someone got stuck inside, before sizing up the fence and concluding that any adult could climb over it with minimal effort.

I bend over, wincing when pain once again shoots up my back, and I squint at the figure; my only light coming from the moon, which is now partially obstructed by clouds.

Recognition sets in.

"Susan Grant?" I speak softly. "What are you doing?"

She doesn't answer.

I lean over the locked gate.

"Susan?" I ask a little louder.

Nothing.

If I go through the effort to hop this fence and this woman is just giving me the silent treatment, I'm going to scream. I'll never admit to anyone how delighted I am at the thought of her having a minor medical episode and me being the hero that saves her life. Could you imagine?

I put my sneaker through a hole in the chicken wire and hoist myself over the white wooden beam on the top. I again place my foot in the chicken wire on the other side to brace myself before jumping down. My shoelace gets caught in the wire and I tumble to the grass below, which hurts more than I'd like to admit. I lean forward to untangle the lace and turn my head back toward Susan as it comes free.

As predicted, I do scream.

Not because I'm angry at Susan.

I scream because Susan is dead.

55

PART TWO:

QUINN

Chapter Seven

There is not a feeling like the hollow ache, deep in my stomach, over facing one of the hardest decisions of my life. Jessie has been the best friend that I've ever had, without question. I never doubted her moral compass for a minute, not until the night I found the smoking gun. The simple pad of paper that instantaneously turned my closest confidant into someone I didn't even know.

Every step of the process is painful. The silent drive to the police station, using my free hand to fold and unfold the sheet of stationary I tore from that pad. The minutes that feel like hours spent in the lobby of the station, wondering if I'm doing the right thing. Admitting to the officer on duty that I'd got it all wrong. I lived through the summer of 1999 at Camp Shady Oaks, researched the events for years, wrote a book about it, and still, I got it wrong. It was my best friend the entire time. Right under my nose. The woman I spend more time with each week than anyone else has been hiding this horrible secret from me and I'm the idiot that never suspected a thing.

Watching Jessie get led away in handcuffs, knowing I'm the only family she's got, and I just gave her up. I'll never again see her without plexiglass between us.

I hear the phone ring and I'm snapped out of my daydream, the one that has become all too common. Overanalyzing all the things I'm going to experience if I do turn Jessie in.

I've been carrying a haphazardly torn sheet of paper from the stationary with me for months. The stationary that changed everything. The 8.5 by 11-inch pastel piece of paper that turned my sweet, kind-hearted best friend into someone capable of murder and framing an innocent person for it, who isn't alive to defend herself. This is the kind of scenario I write about in my novels. I'm trying to think of a solution that wouldn't have me screaming at the absurdity of the story's main character if this *were* a book. If the story is being told from the main character's point of view, how would I even explain that she had no idea her best friend in the world was capable of this? None of her memories from that night make sense anymore. Talk about an unreliable narrator.

The paper is currently folded up in my back pocket and my thumb continues to glide over its edges as I casually hang my hands in my jeans while leaning in the doorway to Jessie's office. I've tried to bring it up so many times; I just can't find the words. I haven't even told Aiden. It's this enormous secret that I've kept from my best friend and my husband and it's eating me alive. I haven't slept a full night since discovering the pad of paper in her office. I wake every morning with the kind of nausea deep in my stomach that comes after a sleepless night. Normally, Jessie is the first person I tell all my secrets to.

"I can't help but notice that Bruce is a little relaxed about the security monitoring since he and Christy started dating. He let a DoorDash driver through the gates today without asking me if I ordered anything first."

"Well, did you?" I ask.

"I mean, it was lunchtime, and I was starving," Jessie responds.

"So, what's the problem?"

"Jessie's just mad because Bruce and Christy are in love and she can't find anyone desperate enough to date her," Aiden says, startling me as he flies by me in the doorway and throws a bright orange slice of cheese at Jessie, which lands with a slapping noise on her desk.

"Piss off, Brooks!" she says with an eye roll, before peeling cheese off the wood in front of her and tossing it in her wastebasket. "Also, you're a millionaire, quit walking around with slices of Kraft cheese. It's fucking weird."

"I'm rich, so it's not weird; it's eccentric," he says with a wink, before giving me a quick kiss on the temple on his way out the door. I fight back a smile.

"I'll keep an eye on Bruce," I tell Jessie. What I *don't* tell her is that, since the threats ceased, I barely feel the need to even have security. The worst kinds of harassment I receive these days is from self-righteous Goodreads reviewers who say I'm overrated and write like a middle school student who got held back three grades. I keep Bruce on the payroll as a favor, and frankly because I like having him around. Since he and Christy began their little love affair, they've both been in a fog of new relationship bliss every day and it's nice being around that kind of positivity. Now that my anxiety is under control, I'm not entirely sure I need Christy, either, but I have no plans to let either of them go.

Neither Bruce nor Christy had taken a real vacation in years, so I strong-armed them into taking a week off this summer. They did a waterfall tour of the Upper Peninsula and had the time of their lives. I couldn't believe how quiet and lonely the house felt without them; even though Aiden lives here now, and Jessie is around most days. I guess I missed the routine.

"Hey, could I talk to you for a minute?" Jessie asks. Her eyes are darting around and she's fidgeting with her hands. *This is it.*

I mentally rehearse the speech I've practiced a thousand times since finding the stationary. I know these conversations never go as planned and I'll probably forget half of my talking points. I realize our relationship will probably be cut into two different distinct chapters: before I hear her confession and after. I'm ready. After this, our lives will never be the same. I close the door behind me, before taking a seat in the leather chair directly in front of her desk.

"Of course, we can talk about anything. You should know that."

I cross my arms over my chest by habit, before registering that this probably makes me seem unapproachable. I want her to feel like she can tell me everything. Every last detail. I uncross my arms and rest my hands on my lap. I try my best not to fidget. I make fierce, compassionate eye contact.

"What's up, Jess?"

"Quinn, you're my best friend. I love you more than I've ever loved anyone. I'd never do anything to hurt you, but I've been keeping a secret from you and it's eating me alive."

Deep breath.

"Okay, I'm sure we can work it out. What did you do?"

She gives a nervous laugh.

"Why do you assume I did something?"

I sit a little straighter.

"Sorry."

"I need you to please just give me a chance to explain myself before you get mad."

"Jess, when is the last time I've gotten mad at anyone around here? C'mon. Spit it out."

She stops picking at her cuticles and places both hands on the desk in front of her before sharply inhaling.

"Quinn, I've been dating your brother. We're in love."

Chapter Eight

"Matt?" I gasp. "He's been divorced for like five minutes. And that's disgusting. And he's my brother!"

The shock of this news makes me forget what I *thought* this conversation was going to be about.

"Well, the divorce has been final for months now and I know you obviously think dating your brother is gross because, well, he's your brother."

How is this somehow worse than anything I prepared for? Matt has the emotional maturity of a six-year-old. He only listens to death metal. He watches slasher films that make *me* queasy, and I write about murder for a living. He drinks beer for breakfast. He absolutely cannot and will not date my best friend.

"Jessie, I don't think you've thought this through."

She gives me a weak smile.

"Jim told me that's exactly what you'd say, and I assure you, I've thought it through."

"*Jim?* My dad knows about this?" I nearly shout. "Please let me get Aiden in here so I can have a voice of reason."

I stand and turn on my heels, pulling the office door open. Aiden nearly falls in, a slight shade of red crawling up his cheeks. He looks at Jessie and she shrugs her shoulders. "I tried," she says.

"Aiden? You knew?" I whisper.

"Babe, give it a chance. They are in love. Who are we to say anything about it?" he asks, placing his hand on my lower back.

I can't believe this. Everyone I love has been conspiring behind my back. I'm the Britney Spears of this household.

"Look, you're both adults. Do whatever makes you happy. I just don't think it's going to end well, and it will make things real awkward at Thanksgiving," I say, before turning to leave.

"You're wrong, I promise you!" Jessie shouts behind me.

The last guy Jess dated was a solidly vanilla man named Tony who worked in tech sales and bored me to tears. He drove a Toyota Corolla and talked endlessly about his Roth IRA and watched Civil War documentaries. How in the hell do you go from that to Matt, who has milk in his fridge that expired two months ago, socks older than me, and watches South Park reruns nightly? I just can't wrap my mind around it.

"Just buzzed your dad in the gate," Bruce says over the intercom.

"Great, just who I wanted to talk to," I mutter to myself, slipping on a pair of shoes and hurrying out the front door to meet him in the driveway.

His aging Chevy truck loudly rumbles as he nears the house. I wouldn't have needed Bruce's warning; I can hear him coming from a mile away. No matter how many books I sell, he refuses to let me buy him a new one. *These new vehicles have all the bells and whistles of a damn spaceship but can't stay on the road for more than a hundred thousand miles before they give the hell up. No thank you.*

He opens the door with his signature thousand-watt smile and singsongs, "Quinnie Q, and how are we doing on this fiiiiiine afternoon?"

"A lot better than you're about to be!" I shout as I meet him at the driver's side door and punch him straight in the arm.

"Who the hell pissed in your Cheerios, little girl?"

"Jessie, dad? My best friend? How could you let Matt talk her into dating him? He's such a creep!"

I see him glance over my shoulder, and I whip around to see Aiden outside the front door, making a rapid cutthroat motion in an attempt to try and warn my dad.

"Both of you! I just can't believe this. We don't keep secrets around here!" I shout. I, of course, have a whopper of a secret and it's directly related to Jessie's whopper of a secret, so I guess this isn't an entirely true statement.

"Quinn Harstead," Dad scolds.

Aiden coughs. I'm technically Quinn Brooks now.

"Oh, you want to claim her when she's acting like this?" Dad asks.

"No, sir," Aiden answers quickly. I scoff.

"Quinnie, this is exactly why we wanted to wait to tell you. Remember when Matty dated the nice young girl you worked with at the movie theater in high school? You nearly blew a gasket."

I stomp my foot and quickly realize how juvenile it is. I double down and stomp the other one.

"Nice young girl? Cari was the most popular girl in school, and she bullied me relentlessly. She locked me in the mop closet for two hours once! Matt betrayed me by dating her! He was sleeping with the enemy!"

My tantrum is interrupted by an old Hank Williams song coming from Dad's ancient cell phone, which is clipped to his waistband. The song I know is assigned to Matt's contact. I leap forward and grab it out of dad's hands as he's answering. I ignore his protests and run a few feet past him, placing the phone to my ear.

"You asshole!" I yell.

"Well, if it isn't my sweet little sister," Matt answers.

"How could you?"

"How could *you*?" he responds.

"How could I what?"

"I don't know, it just seemed fun to turn it back around on you. Hey, let me talk to dad. I'm making a tee time for tomorrow and I need to know when he's free."

"He's retired, he's free all the time," I say before jamming my thumb on the *end call* button.

I march back to dad and hand him back the phone.

"This conversation isn't over," I say, squinting my eyes at him.

"Well, I sure hope not, I just got here," he smiles.

So glad everyone thinks this situation is so damned funny.

I enter the house first, followed by Aiden and dad, and we are greeted by Jessie as we enter the foyer.

"Well, if it isn't my future ex-wife," Dad says, stepping forward to hug her. "Tell Matty he's not the one for you; you've got the wrong Harstead."

"Oh, Jim, I just adore you!" she gushes.

I make an audible sound of disgust before heading to the kitchen and looking at the calendar on my fridge. Tomorrow, Aiden leaves for a two-day tech conference in Cleveland. Christy, my cook Randall, and Bruce all have the day off. Dad and Matt are golfing. This is perfect.

"Hey, Jessie, how about you and I have a girl's day tomorrow? It's been so long."

"This feels like a trap, Q," she says hesitantly.

"No trap, I just probably overreacted today, and I think we could use a day, just the two of us."

"That sounds great!" she says, clapping her hands together.

"Now, that's my girl," dad says condescendingly, rubbing my shoulders. Aiden is also looking at me with pride.

Calm down, idiots. I just need to get her alone to have a talk I've been putting off for way too long. This may be the only time I'm fired up enough to have the courage for a hard conversation.

Bruce interrupts my thoughts with his thunderous voice over the intercom. "Quinn, it's Heather Green for you on the house phone."

I smile. I adore Heather. She probably got my last check and wants to argue about it.

"Heath!" I exclaim, picking up the receiver in the corner of the kitchen.

"Susan Grant is dead."

I laugh.

"Hell yeah, she is! What did she do this time?" I ask.

"No, like actually dead. Susan Grant is dead and I'm the one who found her. I just got back from the police station."

"The police station? How did she die?"

My heart is pounding. This is the last thing Heather needs on her quest for a normal life.

"Quinn, she was strangled."

Chapter Nine

The mysterious deaths, later associated with Mitzi Matthews, followed by her untimely demise at the hands of Heather Green, Delta County's golden child, were the biggest events to happen in this area for decades. Since the news of Susan Grant's body being found by that same golden child, the media is losing their collective minds. Every news outlet in a three-state radius wants a quote from me, the "Queen of Northern Michigan True Crime."

I stare at the 59 unread emails in my inbox and strongly consider clicking two buttons: "select all" and "delete."

My heart breaks for Heather. She had nothing to do with Susan's death, but the media is going to jump at any chance to connect the two. It's only a matter of time before the public finds out about Susan's threats and visit to Heather's house last week.

I close out my browser – I'll deal with this later. In fact, I'll have Jessie handle it for me. She is technically my publicist, after all. A questionably murderous publicist who is dating my only brother, but a publicist, nonetheless.

Before our little day of "fun" begins, I'm sitting cross-legged on the floor of my master bathroom. I've read a lot about the benefits of meditation but can never seem to find the patience to do it myself. Today, I'm giving it the old college try because I need to be level-headed for this discussion with Jessie.

I try to put myself in her shoes. What if I did something horrible when I was sixteen years old and kept the secret for decades? That's a horrible thing to bury deep inside all these years, and I'm sure it's done irreparable mental damage. The truth is, if these events *did* happen just as Jessie described in the fictitious confession letter, I understand her actions. I probably would have done the same thing. Cassie Huntington was a horrible human being; I knew firsthand. People seem to forget in situations like this because you're not supposed to speak ill of the dead and it's just a little easier on everyone involved to say kind things about a person once they're gone. But I was there. She was a nightmare of a person.

I think of what Jessie must have gone through that night, and the idea of her not being able to tell me, her best friend, brings tears to my eyes. I am also somehow grateful that she *didn't* burden me with that information because who knows what my sixteen-year-old brain would have decided to do about it. I feel like I've lived a lifetime since then and am much better equipped to handle the situation now. I just need her to be honest with me.

I breathe in through my nose and out through my mouth. Or is it supposed to be in through my mouth? I know I'm supposed to be doing one or the other. I'm sitting up straight. I need to do this more often; my posture is horrendous from spending so much time on my laptop. Am I supposed to have my eyes open or closed? Dear Lord, I need to clean the jets in my bathtub. Didn't I read something about using baking soda?

Okay, maybe meditation isn't for me.

I hear the chime signaling the front door is open and check my watch; it must be Jessie. I hear her pad up the stairs and kick my door open without warning.

"Yes, hi, I have a date with bestselling author Quinn Harstead," she deadpans, still wearing her dark sunglasses and holding a coffee in each hand.

I roll my eyes and can't help but grin.

"Oh, shut up. Is that coffee for me?"

She reaches forward to hand me the cup and I see by the scribbled writing on the side that it's a pumpkin spice latte. I scrunch my nose; it's still nearly eighty degrees outside.

"What? It's September!" she laughs.

"I'll allow it. Thanks, Jess."

"Remember when Christy wouldn't let you have coffee for like a decade because it made you act like a lunatic?" she says in her signature taunting tone.

"Oh, I'm still a lunatic, I just learned how to hide it from Christy so I can have the good stuff," I say with a wink.

She nods in agreement and sets her coffee on my nightstand before gently leaping in the air and falling on her back in the middle of my king-sized bed. She closes her eyes and exhales before hastily climbing back out.

"Ew, I miss when this was just your bed. I just realized that Aiden is probably naked in here now."

"Yeah, his bare ass is usually right where your head just was," I respond.

I take a sip of my latte and she's right; it tastes like September. This is the last warm week in the forecast and I'm actually looking forward to the colder temps. I had a book signing in Chicago last week and treated myself to a shopping trip on the Magnificent Mile where I bought an embarrassing number of sweaters, but it's been too warm to wear them.

My social anxiety is somehow better in bigger cities because I rarely get recognized. Thousands of people read my books, but I don't let Jessie post many pictures of me on my social media accounts, so most readers have no idea what I look like. The only time I really get attention is in Michigan. I don't mind getting approached in public, it's the ones who don't approach me but whisper loudly and take not-so-discreet cell phone videos of me in line at the deli counter that make me uncomfortable. If they just came up to me, I'd be happy to talk and pose for pictures *with* them instead of just a blurry shot of the side of my face they took without thought.

"So, what's on the agenda for girl's day?" Jessie asks. I requested complete control over today's plans.

"Well, first I have two wonderful ladies coming to the house to give us massages and pedicures. I had Aiden pick up a bottle of champagne before he left so we can make mimosas."

"I love it already," she interjects, excitedly clapping her hands together.

"We'll relax around here for a while before our appointments at three to get our hair washed and styled in Gladstone. I figured we'd catch the new Jennifer Garner movie at five and then we have reservations at The Stonehouse at seven. My brother is going to give us a ride home so we can enjoy some drinks with dinner. Sound good?" I wait to see her reaction to me casually throwing my brother into the plans.

"Matt? He's giving us a ride home?"

"Well, he's giving *me* a ride home. He can take you wherever you'd like."

"Wow, Q. Thank you for being so understanding. You had me a little worried yesterday; I barely slept last night."

Although I'm not exactly thrilled with her behavior lately, this gives me a lump in my throat. I love Jessie and I can't stand the thought of my actions keeping *anyone* awake at night, let alone my best friend. As I lay awake myself last night, I realized I probably was overreacting about Matt. It's just that I don't see the relationship lasting, and a breakup will change everything. I guess we'll burn that bridge when we get there.

Our day goes exactly as I'd hoped. The massage and champagne get her guard down enough to have some honest conversations about how the relationship with Matt began. Apparently, he stopped by one night while Jessie was working late, and Aiden and I were gone to Mackinac Island for the week. His divorce was finalized after months of back-and-forth with their lawyers (would you believe that woman thought she was somehow entitled to some of *my* money? I'm his sister!), and he was feeling a mix of relief and sadness. Jessie tells me that they stayed up half the night talking, and by the time he left, he told her that she helped him feel optimistic about his future for the first time since the split. This makes me quite thankful for Jess. We were all concerned after his wife left him; he barely got out of bed for weeks.

By the time we load into my car to head to our hair appointments, I'm miraculously bordering on acceptance of the relationship. Her eyes light up when she talks about him, and even though he's my disgusting older brother, it's the excitement everyone hopes to see from their best friend. I promise, I'm going to try my best to be kind about the situation. They just better not *dream* of kissing in front of me. I have to draw the line somewhere.

A few hours later, with blow-outs that make us feel like a million bucks (and they nearly cost that; I swear those women charge me more because I have money) and sides that hurt from laughing for two hours at our new favorite romantic comedy, we head to The Stonehouse.

Although it's the nicest restaurant in Escanaba, I don't come here nearly as often as I'd like because it's a bittersweet place for me. Growing up, my father was best friends with Rocky, the owner of The Stonehouse. I called him Uncle Rocky, and he always gave me a fifty-dollar bill for Christmas, which made me feel like a millionaire. My dad spent so much time sitting at the end of the bar "shooting the shit" with him, my mom would call the restaurant phone to tell him it was time for dinner. The old, faded yellow rotary phone would clang and all the regulars would call out, "Time for dinner, Jim!" and belly laugh.

I can't help but look at that barstool as I pass by on our way to the hostess stand. It's now occupied by a man with an expensive suit and a briefcase at his feet. He's ignoring the whiskey glass in front of him while angrily tapping away on his iPhone. Rocky passed away from a heart attack a few years after Mom died and Dad hasn't been back since. This place may have the best food in town, but it will never feel the same again.

"Ahh, Mrs. Brooks. It is such a pleasure to see you, and we are so happy you chose to dine with us tonight! Are we celebrating anything special?" asks the middle-aged woman, who I believe introduced herself as the Front of House Manager last time Aiden and I were in.

I glance at Jessie and smile. "Friendship," I reply. She reaches down and gives my hand a quick squeeze.

The woman, who looks strikingly similar to a young Diane Keaton, leads us to the private room I requested when I made the reservation. It's normally reserved for parties of 8-10, but I offered to pay whatever I needed to for some privacy.

As we are seated, a server shows up to open the expensive bottle of red I requested over the phone. Unscrewing the cork, he pours a sample into Jessie's glass after I motion to defer the first taste.

"Oh, excuse me, I didn't know we were going all out for girl's night!" Jessie laughs, putting her pinkie in the air as she sips the wine.

She nods her approval to the server, and he leaves the room after introducing himself and telling us about the special, which we both ordered without looking at anything else on the menu. The smile on his face tells me he has heard about how I tip and knows he's in for an easy hundred dollars. Those of us who grew up without money and now have an abundance of it seem to be the ones who have *no* issue sharing it.

Jess and I make small talk while devouring our steaks and are on the last few sips of wine when I cash out with the server and ask what time his next reservation in this room is.

"You're the last for the night, Mrs. Brooks."

"Great," I smile, before slapping two extra twenty-dollar bills in the check presenter and asking him for about thirty minutes of total privacy.

He enthusiastically agrees and Jessie looks perplexed. The server leaves, sliding the large banquet room door behind him. She nervously laughs and looks at me, cocking her head.

"Jess, we need to talk," I say, leaning down to grab my purse under the table.

I reach in, retrieve what I'm looking for, and gently place it on the table in front of her. She immediately pales and sits in stunned silence before opening her mouth to speak.

Chapter Ten

"Quinn, I know it sounds cliché, but I can explain."

I nod.

"I was hoping you would, that's why we're here."

Jessie hangs her head and I see a solid trail of tears, tainted black from her mascara, dribble down her cheeks and land on the tablecloth below her. I hand her my burgundy cloth napkin and she slowly reaches her hand up to accept it.

"Jess, you've heard the phrase 'I love you so much, I'd help you hide the body?'"

She nods without speaking and I continue.

"Well, you're my person. You're my best friend. Although I'm sick over what you've done to dishonor Sarah's memory, I'm also so confused and hurt that you didn't feel comfortable telling me. If not me, who?"

Her head snaps up.

"Nobody, Quinn. Nobody knows. I've kept it inside for so long; it has completely controlled my life. Every single day, it's the first thing I think of in the morning and the last thought on my mind as I try to sleep."

I reach forward and grab her hand, before speaking in a low, clear tone.

"Jess, take a deep breath, you need to tell me what happened. All of it."

She stares forward at the closed door and remains silent for a few seconds before flinching as if replaying the scene in her mind. The scene she has tried to forget for decades.

"Well, Q, the longer I lay in bed, the sicker I got with worry over how my parents were going to react over my broken glasses, which I left down by the water. I knew the lenses were shot, but if I could retrieve the frames, maybe they wouldn't be so expensive to replace, and I'd get in less trouble."

I nearly choke on my sobs. I broke her glasses. *I'm* the reason she got back out of bed.

"When I got close to the waterfront, I heard Cassie and Vinny arguing. I stopped to listen for a few minutes, and well…it happened exactly like I wrote, Quinn. I swear. I saw her hit him with the paddle, and I lost my mind. Maybe that's why I sympathized so much with Heather Green; I understand what it's like to lose control of your actions because all you feel is rage. I may have been a foolish teenager, but I hoped to have a future with Vinny. It's all I thought about and she took him from me. I've regretted keeping this a secret from you for so long, but I haven't regretted killing Cassie. Not for a second."

I shake my head in disbelief. I can't grasp that I'm finally hearing these words. These deaths remained a mystery for decades. I was obsessed with finding answers. The deaths of Cassie and Vinny were the reason I lost touch with Aiden. I wrote a book about it, for crying out loud. I wrote a book about an unsolved murder that my best friend committed. It's almost too much to wrap my head around.

"This is why you didn't come to the reunion at Shady Oaks," I say, now realizing that she didn't come because she couldn't bear to go back.

"I'm so sorry for what I've done. I understand if you need to turn me in," she cries, her face crimson red and soaked with tears.

I turn and put both hands on her shoulders.

"Jess, I'd never do that. I'd never, ever do anything to hurt you. I've thought a lot about that night, and I can tell you with near certainty that I would have reacted the same way. I'm just so upset that you involved Sarah."

She's quiet for a moment before looking at me with her swollen, bloodshot eyes.

"Quinn…I am, too. But I need you to know, Sarah knew."

"What do you mean she knew? What does that mean?" I raise my voice louder than intended.

"She caught me sneaking back into the cabin. I was wet and shaking. She turned me around, marched me to the latrines and I told her everything. Well, once I calmed down enough to speak."

I'm stunned. I don't have words.

"She went back to get me a change of clothes and waited until I was done showering. She told me she was going to do everything she could to protect me and that I could never tell anyone, no matter what. I was in shock. I think I finally fell asleep for a few minutes before we were woken up by the commotion. I thought I had dreamed it all until Dave came to tell us about the bodies washing ashore."

She stops for a beat and looks me in the eyes. I can tell there's more. I nod for her to continue.

"Sarah contacted me when the cancer came back. It was her idea for me to write the confession letter after her death. I told her no, and I wasn't going to do it. I still can't believe I did. You can choose not to believe me, but I swear it's the truth."

"Oh, Jessie," I whisper. I lean forward to hug her and we both cry until our bodies don't have the energy to do it anymore.

"Are you going to tell Aiden?" she asks with desperation in her eyes.

Vinny was Aiden's cousin and best friend in the world. I don't think it would be beneficial for anyone involved to tell him now.

"Let's keep this between us for now," I answer.

"Quinn, I feel like an elephant that's been sitting on my chest for over twenty years just got up and walked away. No matter what happens next, thank you."

"You'd do the same for me, I'm sure of it," I say.

We are wiping our tears when Jessie's phone lights up. It's Matt letting us know he's outside to pick us up.

I can't say I'm not a little stung when Jessie takes shotgun, and I am forced to sit in the backseat of my own brother's vehicle.

He turns down the horrible, screaming nonsense that he calls music as we enter the car and smiles like I haven't seen him smile in years.

"Well, if it isn't my girlfriend and my baby sister."

I slam the door shut.

"Shut up and drive, Matt," I say, before staring out the window in silence the entire ride home.

Chapter Eleven

"How's tricks, baby?" Dad asks.

That's his outdated and offensive way to ask how book sales are doing. I've learned to pick my battles with this man.

"They've actually been fantastic this week. Some book reviewer on TikTok did a series on how much she loves my writing and all of my rankings jumped on Amazon."

He takes a minute to ponder this while sliding a pat of butter onto his dinner roll.

"Well, Quinnie, I don't know what Tick Tack is, but I sure hope you mailed her a thank you letter."

I smile.

"You can't ask for people's home addresses these days, dad. But trust me – I sent her a very nice email thanking her for the kind words."

This seems to pacify him.

"That's my girl. How's work going for you, Matty?"

After over a decade on the railroad, my brother quit his job and took a position selling cars at one of the dealerships in Escanaba. I told him I'd find something for him to do around here and pay him well enough to support his Monster energy drink and crusty t-shirt purchases, but he not-so-politely declined. He's not exactly a fan of being known as *Quinn Harstead's brother*. I like to remind him that I spent all four years of high school being referred to as *Matt Harstead's little sister*, so I'm thoroughly enjoying this role reversal.

"I'm not making millions like your favorite child, but I did sell two new trucks and an SUV this week, so life is good, and I can keep the lights on," Matt responds as he shovels pasta in his mouth, splashing red sauce all over the tablecloth in front of him.

"What's the latest with Heather?" Jessie asks. It's still a little weird having her at family dinner as anything other than my friend and employee. She's now Matt's date. I'm doing my best to get comfortable with the idea.

"I just talked to her today. Thank goodness, the city just installed cameras throughout the park and beach area because of vandalism, so she's clearly seen entering the area two minutes before she called the police after finding her body. The scary part is, the time of death was close enough, she could have run into the killer leaving the scene," I explain.

"Well, if they have cameras, can't they see who was by the lighthouse?" Matt asks.

"That's the crazy thing – the cameras are scheduled to be installed on that end of the drive next week. It's almost like somebody knew it was the only place they could remain undetected," I say.

After a beat of silence, Jessie asks, "Do you think it could have been somebody who works for the city? They'd know where the cameras are, and I had a front-row seat for Susan's last few outbursts at city council meetings. She didn't exactly have a lot of admirers."

Jessie has been attending city council meetings on my behalf for the last year. I'm donating money for a drug and alcohol rehabilitation center in Delta County and the proposed site locations have proven to be a hot topic. Everyone wants addicts to get the help they need; nobody wants it to happen in their backyard. Susan Grant had been an incredibly vocal opponent of all three proposed locations, and the idea for a rehabilitation center in general. She's been interviewed by the Daily Press three times and managed to slander my name in each article. She felt those who have lost their way can be healed by the love of Jesus alone and this center would be a waste of money. As I mentioned, it would be *my* money, so I'm not quite sure why she was so concerned. I've toyed with the idea of using my own house, which is in the middle of the woods. Surely, that wouldn't bother anyone, right? Wrong. The hunters came forward and expressed their concern that they might "accidentally shoot one of 'em as they try to escape," as if it would be some sort of maximum-security prison where recovery patients try to saw their way out with a nail file in the middle of the night. I was looking forward to the possibility of donating my house and land to the cause and moving back to civilization. Driving twenty minutes to get groceries or a cup of coffee is starting to wear on me.

"If Heather continues to get questioned, I'll make sure her lawyer knows about the trouble Susan's been causing with the city. You wouldn't mind relaying the information to Doug Angeli, would you?" I ask.

"Of course not," Jessie answers. I'm the only one at this table who now knows why lawyers and police officers have made her uneasy for the last two decades.

"You gonna write a book about it?" Matt asks me.

"Matt, she hasn't even been buried yet. The thought hasn't crossed my mind."

"Liar," he says, taking a swig of his Miller Lite. Dad used to fight him on having a beer with his dinner each night, but he never has more than two, so he also has learned to choose his battles. After talking with his golf buddies about their sons, he knows he could have it much worse.

"What's on the agenda for tomorrow, sweetheart?" Dad asks, taking the napkin from his lap and throwing it on his sauce-filled plate, despite the fact I've told him a million times that it creates a mess when I do laundry. Well, Christy does the laundry, but I imagine it creates a mess.

"I've got to stop by the bookstore in Escanaba and sign their new shipment of my books, I'm dropping in at the radio station to promote 'National Literacy Week,' and then I was thinking I'd grab some D&M Subs on the way home and give Randall the night off."

"Now *that* sounds like a plan!" shouts Randall from the kitchen, where he's washing the pans from dinner.

"Love you, Randall!" I yell back.

"I know you do, Quinn," he responds.

"Do you love me, Randall?" shouts Matt.

"You're all right," Randall says after a pause, and we all smile.

"You guys down for a movie in the theater room?" Jessie asks.

Dad makes some excuse about needing to get home to his dog, and although being the third wheel to my brother and best friend doesn't exactly thrill me, I accept the invitation.

A few hours later, I say goodbye to Jessie and Matt and receive a text from Aiden that he's on his way back from the airport. Today was a good day, and it gives me hope that we can all get along, even with Jessie fitting in the picture as Matt's girlfriend. She hasn't talked to her parents in years, and I know it means the world to her when we include her in our plans as a family. I made a promise a long time ago that I'd do anything to make the rest of Jessie's life easier than it started, and this is simply the next chapter of that agreement.

Chapter Twelve

The ride to downtown Escanaba is just under thirty minutes, which means I can listen to about 75% of my favorite true crime podcast in the car, and just when it starts to get good, I have to park and get out. Although it annoys me every time, it also gives me something to look forward to; the drive home, where I find out who the killer is and how they caught him. I've slowly eliminated dozens of podcasts from my digital library when the attempts at humor and witty banter become too much – just give me the facts, please.

I'm happy to see Heather's car parked behind the bookstore as I slowly pull into the alley. She's been working here part-time, stocking, pricing, and entering books into inventory. It's the perfect job for her; she can get out of the house, make some extra money, and not have to deal with the public.

I park my car next to hers and enter the shop through the aging gray wooden door at the rear of the store. I prefer this entrance because it's discreet and doesn't have a tiny gold bell hanging from the top that announces my arrival.

"Well, if it isn't my golden goose!" shouts Dottie, the elderly owner of Storytime Books. She and her husband opened the place decades ago. Some of my fondest childhood memories are of children's story hour, where I'd sit cross-legged on the floor with the other kids and hang on every word out of Miss Dottie's mouth. My mom would scan the romance section while we learned exactly what happens when you give a mouse a cookie. Dottie's husband, Dan, would give us all Blow-Pops on our way out and shout "Until next time, munchkins!" down the sidewalk as we all got in our parent's cars to leave. Dan passed from a stroke back in 2009, but Dottie doesn't have any plans to close up shop. Each January, she presents me with a plaque, made at the local sports trophy shop, that totals the number of my books sold at her store the previous year. I think it gives her just as much joy to give it to me as it does for me to receive it.

"Well, your golden goose is very excited to see two of her favorite ladies!" I exclaim, holding my hands out in the direction of Dottie and Heather, who is sitting on an oversized cardboard box, fiddling with a pricing gun that appears to be jammed.

"Quinn!" Heather shouts, setting down the gun and walking over to embrace me.

"What's the latest with Susan?" I ask as I slowly pull out of the hug but hold both of her elbows to keep her near. "I've been thinking about you all week."

"That's exactly what we were talking about before you walked in. We never have customers this early, let's go up front and have some coffee so we can properly gossip," says Dottie. If you want to know anything in this town, she's the one to ask. She somehow manages to hear everything, despite never leaving the shop.

For the next hour, we sit in miniature chairs at the children's table up front, drinking our coffee and talking about the rumors surrounding Susan's death while I sign one-hundred copies of my newest book to satisfy the preorders for Dottie's shop.

Although the news of Heather finding Susan's body was the trending topic for days, it appears this town has gained some common sense and very few people seem to think she actually had anything to do with the murder. I don't believe Jess will have to make that call to Heather's lawyer, as the accounts of Susan harassing the members of the city council are already wide enough to cast suspicion on half of them. Much to Heather's delight, Susan also had a falling out with her snooty little bridge club the week before the murder. The suspect list is endless. I'd be lying if I said I wasn't writing the opening to a book in my head while Heather and Dottie tell me about Susan's enemies and frenemies. I still cannot believe we are discussing a murder that happened in Escanaba. The misadventures of Mitzi Matthews were a once-in-a-lifetime chain of events; I never dreamed there would be another homicide while I was still alive to hear about it.

I wind things up with the ladies shortly before 1 pm, as I'm due at the radio station across the street to record some promos. I promise Dottie I'll schedule a signing soon and assure Heather I'll call her to set up a dinner the following week. As I'm walking out the door, Dottie grabs my hand.

"Quinn, I just have to tell you again how proud I am of your success. Even when you were a little girl, I knew there was something special about you. Your mother would be so proud."

I smile and thank her. This is one of those compliments that I'll think about for days and regret not sufficiently communicating how much it meant for me to hear.

The radio promos are awkward, as expected. *This is Quinn Harstead, reminding you to read a book this month, blah, blah, cringe.* I cannot stand the sound of my voice, which is why I don't narrate my audiobooks. It's a fee I'm happy to pay to a trained professional.

I shake it off and take advantage of the overcast day and lack of traffic on Ludington Street by popping in a few shops. Nobody recognizes me, or if they do, they don't say anything. For an entire hour, I go about my business like a normal person, and it feels blissful. By the time I'm done, both hands are filled with shopping bags from locally owned businesses, which makes me feel even better.

I load up my car and drive a few blocks down to D&M Subs to pick up dinner. The two girls working behind the counter squeal when I walk in and gush about my latest novel, which they just finished reading. I answer their questions while they make my order and stay a few extra minutes to take selfies with them and autograph a few napkins, which they assure me they are going to frame when they get home. I'll never get used to this. I throw a hundred-dollar bill in the tip jar on my way out and give them a wink before putting on my oversized sunglasses. Their gasps make me laugh out loud as the door shuts behind me. I miss being that young and excited about everything.

I finish my podcast on the way home (the husband, it's always the husband) and smile when I see four cars lined up in my driveway: Aiden, Matt, Dad, and Jessie. I spent a lot of lonely years out here when I wasn't in a good mental space and having a full table at dinner makes me feel like I can exhale again. It took a long time, but things are finally working out as they should.

The five of us have several different conversations going on simultaneously as we devour our sandwiches. Dad has brought his yellow lab, Bubba, over with him and I'm pretty sure each of us has snuck meat from our sandwiches under the table to him so it's going to be a long night for dad if Bubba's stomach doesn't handle the table scraps. It's a rarity that we are all in jovial moods at the same time, and nobody seems to have anything on their minds other than eating and mindless small talk. Dad even has an extra pep in his step because he finally got a date with Barbara, the owner of a small bakery in town that he's been pursuing all year. Jessie and I have spent the last ten minutes lecturing him on what to wear and begging him to update his cologne from the Calvin Klein Obsession he's been dousing himself with since the early '90s.

Jessie asks if we mind that she leaves her car here so she can ride home with Matt for the night. Despite my best attempt at nonchalance, I flinch slightly when she asks. I swear I'm doing my best to accept this as the new normal, but it's just so strange.

Aiden rubs my back as we stand in the foyer and say goodbye to everyone. Once the door closes behind them, Aiden turns to me and takes my face in both of his hands.

"Quinn, I know. It's weird. But they are in love, and we need to be happy for them. So, do your best, okay?"

I roll my eyes, which makes him cock his head to the right and give me an annoyed schoolteacher *tsk*, but he smiles once I give in and nod my head.

"I'll do my best," I promise.

I'm mildly annoyed when he gently shakes me awake the next morning as the sun is coming up. Today is my day to sleep in and do my writing in the afternoon.

"Babe, wake up," he whispers.

I groan and pull the sheets up over my head. He pulls them back down.

"Quinn, you need to get up."

Panic sets in. *Is it Dad? Did something happen?*

Aiden brushes a few curls out of my face and tilts my chin up.

"The police are here, and they want to talk to you."

Chapter Thirteen

I wrap a plush robe around my shoulders and over my pajamas, throw my slippers on, and hurry down the stairs. I'm still in a half-asleep state of confusion when I see two officers sitting at my breakfast bar and Christy pouring steaming coffee into their mugs.

I recognize Dave Simpkins, whom I interviewed for one of my books. He was the responding officer and the first to arrive on the scene when Mitzi died. Next to him is Officer Larry O'Dell, who has been with Escanaba Public Safety since before I was born. Christy isn't crying, which gives me some hope that this visit doesn't have anything to do with Dad.

"Dave, Larry, to what do I owe the pleasure?" I ask, accepting my own mug from Christy.

"Quinn, I'm sorry we had to drive out here so early this morning, but I needed to ask you a few questions before the news gets ahold of this," Dave says.

"Gets ahold of what?" I ask.

"Were you with Heather Green and Dottie Carlson yesterday?" Larry asks me, setting down his mug and pulling an iPad from his lap before setting it on a small triangular stand on my breakfast bar.

"Yes, I stopped by the store to sign some books and visited with both of them."

"Can you tell me about what time that was?" Dave asks, pulling a pen and pad out of his jacket pocket.

"I probably arrived around 11:30 because we visited for a little over an hour before I had to be at the radio station at one o'clock. What's this about?"

Larry ignores my question and continues with his inquiry.

"And can you tell me where you were around midnight last night?"

I chuckle.

"Well, sleeping. Or attempting to."

"And you, Mr. Brooks?"

"What about me?" asks Aiden.

"Where were you last night?"

He lets out an uncomfortable laugh.

"Sleeping, next to my wife."

"Guys, we will answer all the questions you want, but I think it's only fair you tell us what this is about."

Larry and Dave look at each other before Larry signals for Aiden and me to move closer so we can see his iPad.

"This is Storytime Books security footage from just before midnight last night. Dottie's daughter in Florida called us when she got an alert on her phone from the security app."

Larry leans forward and presses play. We watch as Dottie appears in the frame at the front of the store, which faces Ludington Street. She seems mildly frazzled as she unlocks the door and turns to her right to disable the alarm. She sits on a barstool at the end of the cashier counter and doesn't move again for several minutes. She hasn't turned on any lights in the store and the only reason we can see her is from the light of the moon through the large storefront windows. I glance at the corner of the screen to check the time of the footage. It's now midnight. Dottie's head turns abruptly toward the back of the store. The footage changes to a view of the storage room in the back, where the rear entrance is located. Dottie rushes to the back door, unlatches the deadbolt, and pulls the door open. A figure lunges forward and holds a small towel over Dottie's face. Within seconds, her petite frame falls to the floor and the intruder, clothed entirely in black with a ski mask obscuring their face, grabs her ankles and pulls her out the doorway. The footage stops.

"Oh my god, where did they take her? What are they driving? We have to find her!" I gasp.

"Dottie doesn't have any cameras out back. That's where the footage ends," Dave tells me.

"We have to organize a search immediately," Aiden demands, his hands running through his hair in distress as he begins to pace.

"That won't be necessary," Larry says. "Her body was found on the beach around sunrise this morning by a runner. It appears she was strangled."

I jump back as a mug shatters on the kitchen tile, hot liquid splashing all of us. It takes a minute before I realize that it was the mug I was holding. Christy rushes to tear off sheets of paper towel, handing them to each of the men in the room before attending to me.

"No," I say. "Not Dottie. There's no way."

"I'm afraid so, Quinn," Dave says, his head hanging low. "We searched for her all night after her daughter called the station and sent us the security footage. When the runner called us a few hours later, we knew it had to be Dottie before we even arrived on the scene."

"She couldn't have had that much in the cash register. Most people don't even pay with cash these days. How is that worth a life?" I snap.

Larry hesitates before speaking. "They didn't take anything from the cash register."

"I don't understand. You're telling me this wasn't a robbery? Who in the hell would want Dottie dead? She is a saint!" I say a little louder than intended. "That woman has supported me since I self-published my first book."

I think of her poor daughter, having to watch the footage from thousands of miles away. She must have felt so helpless. I think of all the children who come to Saturday afternoon story hour. How will their parents ever explain? I think of Heather Green, her favorite employee.

"Have you told Heather?"

"We have two officers at her house now," Larry answers.

I grab my keys from the counter. I need to make sure she's okay. That woman has already experienced enough loss for a lifetime.

What Aiden says next stops me in my tracks.

"I don't understand. Susan and now Dottie – it's all so random. Do you gentlemen think we have some sort of serial killer on our hands?"

Midnight in Delta County

PART THREE:

QUINN AND HEATHER

Chapter Fourteen

Meryl is sitting on the couch next to Heather, rubbing her back, when the doorbell rings. She's on her feet to answer it before Heather realizes her hand is no longer there. Being in a daze would be putting it mildly; Heather loved Dottie like a mother. She's the only one in town that would hire her after her release from jail.

"Heath," Quinn says breathlessly as she pushes past Meryl and wraps her in her arms.

"Not every day a famous author shows up in her bathrobe and flannel pajamas. I'll put on a pot of coffee," Meryl quips.

Quinn glances down at herself and gives a tight smile, shaking her head. "As soon as the cops told me the news, I just grabbed my keys and hopped in the car. I can't believe I left the house like this."

She squeezes Heather's hands, and despite only knowing her for a couple of years, Heather can read her mind. She can't believe this is happening to her, of all people. She's once again surrounded by untimely death.

"How are you," she says, more of a statement than a question because she already knows the answer. Not well.

"I just don't understand. The cop said nothing was taken. Why would anyone do this to Dottie?" Heather asks.

"I don't know, but I promise I'm going to do everything in my power to find out who did this. I'm going to call the station and see if they'll let me put up a reward for information," Quinn says.

"Don't you think they'll criticize you for not also coughing up money for information on Susan's death?" Meryl asks from the kitchen.

Heather smiles as Quinn rolls her eyes.

"Well, damnit, I guess I'll do the decent thing and offer a reward for both. Even though Susan was a pious lunatic who threatened your niece and me with eternal damnation on numerous occasions."

Meryl snorts.

As soon as they all settle in with their coffee, there's another knock at the door. Heather's eyes shoot to the clock above the stove; she can't believe it's already time for Ryan to drop Evie back off before he heads to work. Although he has the decency to knock, he never waits for one of them to answer, he just comes right in.

"Good morning, ladies!" Ryan loudly whispers as he enters the living room with a sleeping Evie in one arm and her favorite stuffed elephant wrapped around the other. "Oh, and Quinn Harstead. In her pajamas? Are you just overly exhausted from trying to ruin my life?"

Ryan isn't Quinn's biggest fan. After *Revenge and Murder in Delta County* came out, readers were calling for Ryan's head on a platter. Well, more accurately, another part of his anatomy. Heather somehow had minimal backlash for her manslaughter charge, but Ryan's shocking infidelity made him a target for scorned women everywhere. Quinn only told the truth, it's not her fault the women of America turned on him.

"I'll take Evie," Meryl says with her hands out and nods her head towards the chair next to Heather, motioning for Ryan to sit.

"What's going on?" he asks.

"Dottie Carlson was murdered last night," Heathers says.

"What? What do you mean? How?"

"It appears she was strangled and that's all we know," Quinn answers, although the question wasn't directed at her. "I stopped by the shop yesterday and visited with her and Heather for a while, so the cops showed up at both of our houses this morning."

"They don't think you guys had anything to do with it, right?" he asks, wide-eyed.

"I highly doubt it. They said they think she was murdered just after midnight," Heather says.

"That's around the same time Susan was killed, right?" he asks, and Quinn and Heather sharply turn their heads toward each other. They can't believe they didn't put this together before now. "What are the chances this town has two murders, both victims are older women who were strangled, and both killed at or around midnight?"

The women sit in silence. How did Heather's ex-husband piece this together immediately when it hasn't occurred to either of them all morning?

"Anyway, I've got to head to the office. Sorry for your loss. Both of you," he makes a quick nod to Quinn before cordially patting Heather on the shoulder and leaving.

"He sure is a handsome bastard," Quinn mumbles once he's out the door. "But I wonder if he was born without an ounce of empathy, just like his mother."

"You might be onto something there," Heather responds.

Meryl reenters the room moments later with Evie on her hip. She's sleepily holding a bottle and staring at Quinn; someone she's not used to seeing in her house.

"Hello, my sweet baby," Heather smiles as Meryl hands her over. She continues to stare at Quinn and reaches out a little hand in her direction.

"Well, this is a first," Quinn responds. She's not a fan of children, but she can't help but smile. Evie has that effect on people. Quinn holds out her pointer finger in Evie's direction and she wraps her sweet little fingers around it. Evie drops the bottle from her hand, which lands in Heather's lap, and starts speaking in gibberish to Quinn.

"She likes you," Heather says with a smile.

"You're not so bad yourself," Quinn tells her.

They spend the next few moments fussing over Heather's precious daughter before she inevitably brings up what is dancing around in both of their minds.

"So, once this news breaks, it's going to be a zoo around here."

"Why don't both of you come out to my house for a few days until it blows over? I've got two empty guest rooms and plenty of food," Quinn offers. "I've never had a baby in the house, Christy will be beside herself."

Heather's first instinct is to refuse, but something in her wants to take Quinn up on the invitation. She's never seen Quinn's house, and she knows Meryl is dying to see the inside. Heather looks at Meryl and she gives a non-committal shrug, but her eyes are pleading with her to say yes. The ladies in her cribbage group will be hanging on every word when she gets back and tells wild stories about her time at the mansion in the woods.

"You know what? We'd love to. Thank you so much for the offer. Give me an hour or so to pack up some things and we'll head that way."

Quinn's eyes light up, which tells the women she genuinely does want them to come and wasn't just offering to be polite.

"I'll have Randall cook the best dinner of your lives, and we can watch a movie in the theater room, whatever you guys want!" she exclaims.

"Theater room?" Meryl can't help herself.

"I've been rich too long, haven't I?" Quinn laughs.

"You won't hear us complaining!" Meryl responds.

Before Quinn leaves, Heather mentions that she wants to give Frank a call to get him up to speed, and she's going to shoot Ryan a text to let him know she'll be taking Evie out to Quinn's.

"You get Evie packed up, I'll handle calling Frank," Mer says nonchalantly, before leaving the room with her cell phone in hand, flipping it open to punch in Frank's number because she still hasn't figured out how to store a contact and refuses all offers of assistance.

Heather's lips curl into a smirk and she shakes her head.

"What's that about?" Quinn asks as she stands to leave.

"We'll have plenty of time the next few days for me to catch you up on all the mundane gossip around here."

"I seriously cannot wait," Quinn responds, and Heather believes her.

She certainly didn't have "avoiding media attention from the news of a possible serial killer by hiding out at Quinn Harstead's mansion" on her list of plans for getting her life back on track but, alas, her life never does seem to go according to plan.

Chapter Fifteen

It's not that tonight's Harstead family dinner was dysfunctional or even eventful; it was just odd. The dynamic between these seven adults, one baby, and Randall (who was *living* for the possibility of drama) was uncomfortable at best.

Between courses of butternut squash bisque and pot roast (Randall's cooking has gone *full* autumn, despite the unseasonably warm temps), Quinn sat in silence as she watched the interactions between these near strangers. Her father alternated his flirtatious comments between Heather and her Aunt Meryl. Jessie seemed inexplicably jealous of the attention these ladies were getting from Jim. Most surprisingly, Aiden focused solely on Evie, whom he bounced on his lap while ignoring his dinner. Yes, her dear husband, who continues to vehemently deny ever wanting a child in their lives, is now utterly smitten with the soon-to-be one-year-old.

Matt seems oblivious to Jessie's desperate desire to regain his father's admiration and instead is entirely transfixed on the pecan tart Randall just delivered to the table.

"Aiden, why don't you let me take her so you can enjoy some dessert?" Heather asks, holding her arms open to accept Evie.

"Nonsense. I'm sure you miss plenty of hot meals as a single mother," Aiden answers. He takes a small spoonful of Evie's pile of mush and makes airplane noises as his arm glides through the air and the baby's giggles are enough to make everyone at the table smile.

"You've got a good man," Heather tells Quinn.

Quinn rubs Aiden's arm to show the rest of the table that she knows what a good man he is, but she's also quietly a little annoyed at this sudden behavior change. Aiden rarely pays attention to any child in the room, and he even stepped back from being involved in operations at Camp Shady Oaks when the rambunctious pre-teens became a little too much. He's still President of the organization that operates the camp, but his involvement is almost entirely financial. Quinn worries that his change in demeanor toward babies is going to make everyone think that *she's* the reason they aren't having children when it's very much been a unanimous decision.

Quinn leans back in her chair, which gives her a direct line of vision into the kitchen. She catches Randall's eye and gives him a wink, which is the signal to wrap things up and help get her guests out of there. They agreed upon this gesture last year when Aiden's extended family came to town for an early Thanksgiving celebration and differing political opinions became the not-so-pleasant topic of discussion. Once Randall reappeared in the dining room and began clearing plates, everyone seemed to take the hint and began saying their goodbyes. Unbeknownst to Aiden, Quinn snuck back into the kitchen that night while Randall was cleaning up and they decided that having a secret signal was necessary now that Quinn was beginning to have people in her home again, people that might overstay their welcome.

Jessie, Matt, and Jim were rising from their chairs before Randall had the last of the plates cleared. Quinn gave herself a mental reminder to significantly increase his Christmas bonus this year.

"So, Jessie and your brother? That's a little unexpected, yeah?" Heather asks Quinn after getting Evie to sleep in one of the guestrooms.

"Unexpected would be putting it lightly," Quinn mumbles as she inserts her electric corkscrew into a bottle of Cabernet.

Quinn was delighted to see Meryl's excitement over the spa-like amenities at her house. It also made her somewhat disappointed in herself that she's gotten used to this life of luxury, something she never dreamed would happen after her modest upbringing. After enjoying an after-dinner sauna session to "burn the calories from all the delicious food that damn chef forced on us," she then selected a single-use mud mask packet from the guest bathroom and is currently soaking in the jacuzzi tub, with one of the *Real Housewives* shows playing on the small flatscreen in the corner of the bathroom. Randall generously made her an after-dinner cocktail to take with her. Both women knew they wouldn't be hearing from Mer for a while.

"It's a nice night, want to sit outside for a while?" Quinn asks as she fetches two wine glasses down from the cupboard. "Aiden is in work mode; he'll probably be on that computer half the night."

"I'd love to. I brought the baby monitor in case Evie fusses," Heather responds.

"Let her fuss, Aiden will probably handle it himself at this point," Quinn quips.

Heather gives a quick laugh before saying "I couldn't believe how good he was with her at dinner. I had no idea he was into babies."

"I learn something new about that man every day," Quinn gives a tight smile.

There is something about the kind of intoxication that comes from sharing an expensive bottle of wine with a friend under the stars that makes you lose just enough good sense to say things you normally wouldn't dream of.

In addition to mild insults about her husband's commitment to work, Quinn dances around the idea of telling Heather all her secrets. She's not sure what it is about her, but she feels like she could trust her with the deepest, darkest ones.

Heather opens the door by telling Quinn about her questionable feelings toward Mitch. She appreciates that Heather doesn't apologize for it, she simply states how she's feeling and admits she doesn't know if it's a good idea to start a new relationship with everything going on in her life. She also notices a slight twinkle in her eye when she talks about him, but nowhere near the smile that's plastered on her face as she details her theories about Meryl and Frank being secretly in love. Quinn laughs so hard she cries when Heather tells her the lengths the two have gone to hide their flirtation.

As she pours her third glass, Quinn does the unthinkable. She tells Heather the biggest secret she holds.

Jessie's secret.

It's out of her lips before she can stop the words from spilling out.

It may be the wine or the light of the full moon playing tricks on her, but Heather Green does not seem very surprised to hear that Jessie is the Shady Oaks killer.

Quinn attempts to backtrack her betrayal by adding "I can't tell you I wouldn't have made the same decision in her position."

"Oh, you and I both," Heather responds. "If that night played out exactly how Jessie told you it did, I really place very little fault on her. From everything I heard, Cassie Huntington was a monster and I absolutely believe she attacked Vinny. The important part of this discussion being *if* these events happened as Jessie described."

Quinn gives her a look of confusion.

"Jessie obviously has gone great lengths for decades to cover her tracks and make sure nobody can ever pin one or both of the deaths on her."

Quinn, still confused, says "Yes, I suppose she has."

Heather continues.

"So, that janitor who everyone suspected, I can't think of his name…"

"Jack," Quinn volunteers.

"Yes, Jack. The man whose future was so bleak that he took his own life and became the top suspect for decades. Who is to say Jessie didn't kill him and make it look like a suicide?"

Quinn sits up straight.

"Heather, she was sixteen years old."

"My friend, I think she quit being sixteen the minute she held another girl's head underwater until she stopped breathing."

The truth is, until this very moment, Quinn never considered the possibility Jessie had anything to do with Jack's death. He was a sad, desolate man who never got over the death of his brother and took his own life at the very camp that claimed his brother's decades earlier…right?

Chapter Sixteen

Quinn couldn't stop watching Jessie from the corner of her eye as the choir sang "Ave Maria."

She's been Quinn's best friend for decades. She brought her anything she needed during her recluse years and never once judged her for her fear of going outdoors. She felt more like a sister than a friend, and now she was in love with Quinn's brother, which brought her a step closer to *actually* being a sister. Despite some drunken suspicions that seemed incredibly feasible when initially presented, the light of day and soberness of the morning now told her she was wrong. There is no way Jessie was capable of killing someone without provocation. Much like Heather, Jessie is a morally sound person who regrettably lost control once in her life. Quinn was willing to bet her life on the fact that Jessie would never lose control like that again, but it didn't stop her from examining her eyes as she watches the pallbearers carry Dottie Carlson's casket down the aisle of the church.

Jessie only had the pleasure of meeting Dottie on a couple of occasions, usually during Quinn's book signings, but she was impacted by the woman's kindness and admiration for Quinn. Any friend of Quinn's was a friend of Jessie's. She watched a solemn tear drop from Jessie's eye as the procession passed their pew. She shed a few of her own when she caught sight of Dottie's daughter, Beth. The pain in her eyes made Quinn's breath catch in her throat. She thought of her own mother's funeral. Although she was only thirteen, she knew her life would never be the same.

Dottie's extended family stood outside the church to thank the attendees and accept countless declarations of thoughts, prayers, and stories of Dottie's generous and kind nature.

Since Quinn, Jessie, Heather, and Meryl were sitting near the front of the church, they were among the last to exit. Camera bulbs flashed aggressively as Quinn and Heather exited the church.

"I'm so sorry for this," Quinn said to Dottie's daughter Beth as they approached her in the line. She felt the heat coming to her face and willed it to stop. She shouldn't be embarrassed; she's done nothing wrong. "There's no good way to pay my respects to your mother without these animals hounding me."

Beth assured Quinn she understood. She took her and Heather by the hand and squeezed them tight.

"My mother thought the world of you both. She would just light up when telling me about Quinn's new novel or how well Heather is adjusting. She loved you guys."

"The feeling was very, very mutual. She was a mother figure to us both, and lord knows we needed one," Heather responds.

The ladies greet the rest of Dottie's grieving family, doing their best to ignore the flashbulbs and shouts for a comment. It made them keenly aware of how Delta County residents probably feel about news outlets being in their sleepy town again so soon after decades of peace and quiet. The entire town thought the death of Mitzi Matthews would be their last dance with national news for a very long time.

Heather elbows Quinn and nods toward the street in front of them. Two unmarked cars are parallel parked with three men in suits leaning on the driver's side doors. All three are wearing aviator sunglasses and have their arms crossed over their chests. Although they spend an extra beat staring at the two women, they continue to scan the crowd. Quinn and Heather both know they are detectives, and they are looking for anyone unusual at Dottie's funeral service. There are also two cameramen filming everyone leaving the church. Neither of them is wearing any press credentials, which means they are probably working for the investigators. Quinn pictures the officers spending hours in a dark room, reviewing the footage and trying to identify anyone suspicious, just like they do in the movies.

Heather replays the details of the crimes over and over in her head, hoping to find any explanation other than a serial killer. Maybe it's just the biggest coincidence in history that both women were killed at the same time in the same manner. Maybe they aren't related at all.

Whether it's the work of a serial killer or just two random killings, the same question is on everyone's mind: will there be more victims before it's over?

Chapter Seventeen

For weeks, nothing happens. No more victims, no new suspects, and no real progress in the investigation.

The only additional information released by the police is the confirmation that both women were killed at or around midnight and the fact that both of their cell phones are missing. According to records from their service providers, both women's phones pinged the tower closest to where their bodies were found before being turned off. Both women lived alone and were not known to be out of the house so late at night. Dottie's case was particularly peculiar, as she seemed to be entering the bookstore with a purpose as if someone asked her to meet there at such an hour.

Every conversation at each restaurant, bar, or coffee shop in the entire county revolves around the deaths of Susan and Dottie. How could it not? This isn't Chicago and it certainly isn't Detroit. Quaint little Delta County could have an actual serial killer on the loose. For the first time in their lifetimes, families begin locking their doors. Children have to be home before dark. The city council receives several requests from concerned parents to cancel trick-or-treating this year. Nobody feels safe.

On the last Saturday of September, Heather steps outside her patio doors and finds Meryl wrapped up in a red flannel blanket, drinking coffee on the back deck with a Sudoku puzzle in her lap. Fall has arrived overnight. The air is crisp and burns Heather's nostrils briefly when she takes her first deep breath of the morning. Leaves are quietly falling from the two towering trees in her back yard and the steam from Meryl's coffee steadily rises from her oversized mug. These are the mornings Heather used to dream of when she was locked in a windowless cell. The mornings she vowed to never again take for granted. She'd love to feel the magic of the changing seasons this morning, but all she feels is dread.

Everyone is waiting for the next victim to be discovered. It's not a matter of if, but when. The entire town is convinced there's a killer in their midst. The Delta County Strangler: that's what the locals are calling him. Or her.

Heather fakes a smile as she says good morning to Mer and grabs her mug to top off.

"I wasn't sure fall was coming this month, but here she is," Meryl says, holding her hands up in the cool morning air.

"Here she is," Heather repeats with a smile as she turns to reenter the house and pour herself a cup. Ryan has Evie for the weekend and will drop her back off Sunday night. Heather has nothing on the agenda until then.

Dottie's daughter, Beth, would like to keep the bookstore open and offered Heather the position of manager since she can't operate it herself from Florida. Heather asked her for a week to think it over, but she's fairly sure she's going to decline the offer. Everything in that store, from the ancient wooden shelves to the off-brand powdered creamer at the coffee station reminds her of Dottie. She also knows that running the store would mean having to interact with the public, something she was happy to avoid as the part-time inventory girl.

Coffee in hand, she takes a seat on the outdoor couch and breathes deeply. She reminds herself, for the millionth time, that there is nothing she can do about the murders other than keep herself and her family safe. She has been locking every door, she purchased an extra pepper spray, and she even asked Jim Harstead if he'd show her how to shoot a gun, to which he enthusiastically agreed. There's nothing more she can do.

Her phone vibrates with a text from Mitch. Although they've chatted a few times, she hasn't seen him in person since the night they visited on her front porch, right before she took a leisurely midnight walk and discovered a dead body.

Donuts?

The text is below a picture of Mitch with a Donut Connection box balanced on his head. Heather smiles.

Sounds great. My house?

The minute she presses send, the side gate to her house bangs open and Mitch comes jogging in with his case of donuts and a victorious smile on his face.

"What if I had said no?" she asks.

"Who says no to donuts?" he responds, before setting them on the outdoor table and leaning to greet Meryl and kiss her cheek.

"You ladies need to start locking that gate. Haven't you heard there's a killer on the loose?"

Meryl gives Heather a dirty look. They've discussed the importance of keeping the gates locked and Heather was the last to use it, the night before when she watered the plants at dusk. She ignores Meryl and thanks Mitch for the suggestion.

"You're awfully chipper this morning," Meryl tells him as she takes her first bite and a glob of red jelly drips down her chin. Mitch hands her a napkin from the stack he has folded into his jacket pocket.

"Fall is in the air. How can that not put a little pep in your step?"

"It's a little hard to celebrate anything when we could all be strangled at any moment," Heather deadpans.

"If it makes you feel any better, I was at the station yesterday and they gave me the distinct impression that they had some serious leads," Mitch tells the women.

"Why were you at the station?" Heather asks.

"Susan and Dottie both had all their insurance policies through me, so the cops had a few questions."

"Oh my god, are you a suspect?" Heather gasps.

"No, Heath, I wasn't the damn beneficiary of their policies, I just administered them. Jesus."

"Oh," she sits back in her chair.

"I think they are just trying to find anything the women had in common. I know your dickhead ex-husband was their doctor, so I'm sure he'll get questioned, too."

"Yes," Meryl adds, "Frank represented them both in legal matters in the past. He was questioned last week."

Heather huffs. "It's Escanaba; if they want to interview everyone they had in common, they are going to have to bring in the whole town."

"How is Quinn feeling about all of this?" Mitch asks.

Heather thinks it's a little random for Mitch to ask about Quinn.

"I mean, she hopes the killer or killers get caught soon, just like the rest of us. She loved Dottie. What made you ask about her?" Heather asks.

"I'm sure everyone is exaggerating the coincidences, but I was just curious to hear what she had to say about it."

Heather wrinkles her nose and looks at Meryl, who just shrugs.

"Mitch, what are you talking about?"

Mitch stops mid-bite.

"Her book…you know, the one you were reading the last time I saw you?" he says, tilting his head.

"I've been busy, I've only read one chapter. What about it?"

"People are saying the killings kind of sound like the plot of the book. I mean, the damn thing's called *Midnight*, and that's apparently when the murders happened. Kind of a coincidence, eh?"

Heather's heart is beating so loudly, it's reverberating in her ears. Is this why Quinn is getting so many requests for a comment from the media? Is this why she hasn't wanted to leave the house in weeks and advised Heather to do the same? Heather feels like a horrible friend for not reading the book, but her mind has been all over the place and each time she sits down and opens the book, she dozes off. She's a mother; she's exhausted.

"A random killer copying the plot of a bestselling book? That stuff happens in a bad episode of *Law and Order*, not in small-town Michigan. There's no way," Heather says, willing herself to believe the words.

"Calm down, Matlock. I'm just telling you what people are saying. Some conspiracy theorists are suggesting she might have had something to do with it so she can sell more copies of the book."

"Well, people are idiots," Heather responds, not entirely convinced this is a theory she needs to be dismissing so quickly. "Maybe I'll take a look at the book later. I'll let you know what I think."

"I'm always interested to hear what goes on in that brain of yours," Mitch smiles, before shoving the last bite of donut in his mouth. "Ladies, I'd love to stay and visit, but I've got places to be. I'll hit you up later, Heath."

Despite her nonchalance, she runs inside to grab the book in question the minute Mitch leaves. She pulls a throw blanket off the couch and settles outside on the deck to dive in.

"Give me the cliff notes, will ya?" asks Meryl before returning to her Sudoku puzzle.

Heather can't turn the pages fast enough. Not only is she anxious to get to the murders that apparently happen in the book, but she's also completely enthralled by the story. Damn, Quinn Harstead can write a mystery. She once again kicks herself for not reading this earlier.

Other than going in the house a few times to use the bathroom and grab snacks, Heather's only interruption occurs when she texts Ryan to check on Evie. He responds with a picture of her playing in the leaves in their front yard, which comforts her enough to set her phone down and return to the book.

"Dinner?" Meryl peeks her head out of the patio door and nearly knocks Heather out of her seat.

"Damn, Mer, you scared the shit out of me!"

"Kid, you've had your face in that book all day. Come up for air."

Heather reluctantly sets the book down and stands up to stretch. The sun is beginning to set, and the first mosquito of the night has announced its arrival by biting her in the upper thigh, right through her leggings.

"It's so good, Mer. Now I get why she's sold so many copies. I can't put it down."

Meryl holds up three menus for local restaurants. Heather chooses one and points to the giant wet burrito on the second page.

"I'm going to need sustenance to finish this book tonight."

"Well, shoot, I guess you should mix up a pitcher of margaritas as long as we're having Mexican food. I'll go pick it up."

Heather smirks. Meryl likes to act as if it's someone else's fault that she's forced to have a drink with dinner.

Thirty minutes later, Mer is back with three burritos and enough chips and queso to feed a small village. Heather sets the table, complete with the requested margaritas, and laughs when she sees the amount of food for the two of them.

"I guess we're having leftovers tomorrow?" she says with a smile, just before the doorbell rings. She arches her eyebrow. "You are expecting someone?"

The visitor doesn't wait for Meryl to get to the door before easing it open.

"Yoohoo!" yells Frank. He comes into the kitchen with an expensive bottle of tequila tucked under his arm. "Your Aunt Mer says you make the margaritas a little weak there, kid. No offense."

Since when does Meryl not mention that Frank is coming over? Since when does she not mention that they've even talked today? Heather begins to question whether Meryl *did* mention these things while she was completely absorbed in Quinn's novel. She distinctly remembers Mer peeking her head out the door several times, Heather nodding each time to satisfy whatever she was needing.

"Frank, what a nice surprise," Heather says, reaching down for a third plate and margarita glass.

"For Christ's sake Heath, I told you he was coming over so you could debrief us on this little book. We're dying to hear about it."

"Sorry, I guess I was lost in the pages. Have a seat, Frank," Heather says before setting the plate and glass in front of the seat opposite Meryl's.

Over dinner, Heather fills them in on everything she's read so far.

The story, set in the next town over Gladstone, centers around a character whose life eerily resembles Heather's. She was Homecoming Queen and Captain of the cheerleading squad before a tragic housefire takes the lives of her entire family. Decades later, she finds out the fire wasn't an accident. It was set intentionally by a man who believed she was in the house. Several murders occur in town and all the victims are connected to the main character. Each victim's time of death is estimated to be around midnight and the authorities think that the man, who has been on the run, is killing people close to the main character to frame her, as her midnight alibis aren't exactly airtight. Her name is Malorie and Heather is currently reading about how the murders are beginning to make her go crazy. She can't bear the thought of another person losing their life just because of their connection to her.

They all agree that Quinn may have taken a page from Heather's own story to create the character of Malorie, but they're sure all authors do that to the people in their lives. She only has five or six chapters left to read, but so far, the only real-life similarities are that the victims were strangled, their cell phones are the only items missing, and the crimes occurred sometime within the midnight hour. Sure, Heather knew both victims just like Malorie in the book, but it's a small town. It would be very unlikely for Heather *not* to know someone here.

"So, who is this guy committing the crimes?" Frank asks before dripping queso all over his chin. Mer grabs a napkin from the center of the table and leans forward to wipe it for him. Heather notes how comfortable she looks doing this.

"That's the thing," Heather says. "They haven't specifically said who this guy is or why he's doing it. At this point, the reader just knows that Malorie figured it out. She hasn't even gone to the cops yet."

Frank and Mer seem to chew on this for a minute.

"So, these idiots who think Susan and Dottie's deaths are related to the book. In theory, they believe someone is killing them to frame...*you?*" Meryl asks.

"I'm not sure, the first time I have even heard about the book being discussed in town was from Mitch today. I can't see how someone could say I'm being framed for the murders -- the cops even told me I'm not a suspect. Mitch hinted that the people in town think Quinn could have something to do with it, which is nonsense."

They sit in silence for a moment before Frank changes the subject to the upcoming UPtoberfest in the park, but they are all wondering the same thing: is it possible someone is trying to copy the plot of the book? They all alternate between curiosity and back to disbelief because the idea is just too ludicrous to consider.

Later that night, Heather is sitting on the couch with her feet kicked up, a hot mug of tea in one hand and *Midnight* in the other. Meryl enters the living room just as Heather finishes the final chapter. She closes the book, sets it in her lap, and stares straight forward.

"Well?" Mer asks.

"It was the main character the whole time. Malorie. She was the killer."

Chapter Eighteen

Vicki is twirling her pen between her fingers like a baton and Quinn finds it not only distracting but inappropriate. She follows Quinn's eyes, and with a slight look of embarrassment, sets the pen down.

"So, is it your belief that there is a crazed maniac on the loose, reenacting scenes from your book, or just a few coincidences that have people grasping at straws to liken your book to the tragedies that happened in Escanaba?"

Quinn considers this for a moment. Either option is enough to make her lose sleep at night.

"Well, for example, you know the scene in *Midnight* when Jackie is walking at Van Cleve Park?"

Vicki doesn't break eye contact often, but she does as soon as the question is out of Quinn's mouth. Quinn gasps, while also barely managing to hold back a smile.

"Vicki! You haven't read the book!"

Vicki opens her mouth to explain, but Quinn interrupts.

"Wait, have you read *any* of my books?"

"Of course, I have," Vicki says quickly.

"Oh really, which one was your favorite?" Quinn tests her.

"Quinn, we aren't here to talk about me and my reading habits. You are paying good money for a one-hour session where we discuss *your* life and *your* feelings."

Quinn can't explain why, but this pleases her to no end. Any lingering doubts about Vicki's intentions are erased. She made a small fortune off Quinn during the years she was afraid to leave her house; a $100 surcharge was added to every visit made to her home. All those years of counseling and Vicki has not once been curious about Quinn's writing? She could have made Vicki the murderer in her last novel, and she'd never even know about it. She's delighted at this news and the fact that it's making Vicki uncomfortable is just a bonus. *Nothing* makes Vicki uncomfortable.

"Now, tell me why you think Heather is upset with you," Vicki changes the subject.

"Well, much like yourself, I don't think Heather had read the book before the murders happened."

Quinn can't help but smile while saying this. Vicki ignores it.

"Okay, so what is the issue?"

"There was a night and day change in her voice when I called her yesterday. She asked me a few details about the book for the first time, so I think she just read it. My guess is that she heard people discussing the similarities and her curiosity got the best of her."

Vicki writes this down. Quinn hates when Vicki writes things down, it drives her absolutely insane not to know the reason why. Of all the things she says in the span of an hour, what determines the bits of information that are worthy of being recorded in her little leather-bound notebook?

"Why would this make her upset with you?" Vicki asks.

"Well, the main character has some similarities to Heather. Her name is Malorie, and spoiler alert here, she ends up being the killer…hiding in plain sight the entire novel."

"The main character ends up being the villain. Now, that's a twist. I see why it's been so popular."

"Not popular enough to end up on your nightstand," Quinn winks. This time, although brief, Vicki visibly squirms.

"So, you're under the impression Heather is upset with you for writing this character. Have you considered asking her about it?"

Quinn shakes her head.

"My relationship with Heather has been pretty harmonious. I write a book convincing the nation that they shouldn't be upset with someone convicted of manslaughter, I quietly send her a few bucks, and we text each other memes and check in occasionally. It's nice. I'd rather not change anything."

"You come here for advice, Quinn. My advice is that you sit down and talk to her about it. I know you'll feel a lot better if you do."

Vicki quickly glances at the clock above Quinn's head, which signifies that their time is up. Quinn stands to leave, and as she bends down to grab her bag, she smiles at Vicki one last time.

"Yes, I do come here for advice because you're so good at giving it. Thank God I don't come for book club discussion, yeah?"

Vicki opens her mouth to protest but decides against it and shakes her head as Quinn laughs the whole way out of her office.

Chapter Nineteen

"You want to go for their eyes, Heath," Frank says, lifting two fingers to demonstrate. He jabs them forward in such an awkward motion, Heather can't help but laugh.

"I'll be sure to gouge 'em right out," she assures him.

They are twenty minutes deep in a discussion about self-defense when Frank finally lets up and takes a seat on the couch.

"That lesson must have been exhausting. You want a pop?" Meryl asks from the kitchen.

"That'd be great, Mer," he answers.

Heather is slightly annoyed she didn't get offered a cold beverage; she's the one who has had to play the role of a captive audience while Frank states and repeats the most basic survival advice three to four times before he's satisfied that Heather has retained the information. Her annoyance fades when Meryl enters the room with two cold cans of Vernors.

"Did you give your presentation to Julie yet?" Heather asks, only half teasing. The woman who is in co-charge of her infant daughter two days a week better know how to protect her.

Frank gives an indifferent shrug.

"Frank, you don't have to pretend not to like her for my sake. What's done is done," Heather says, patting his shoulder for reassurance.

"My dear, for once, it has nothing to do with you. I didn't warm up to Julie in the decades she spent in our lives before my son decided to ruin his family and I just can't manage to warm up to her after. I'm giving it my best."

Heather is still surprised by the level of support Frank has given her. She knows that people often choose sides when a couple divorces, but she never imagined her father-in-law would choose hers over his own son. He still spends time with Ryan and includes his son Hunter when appropriate, but he enjoys his visits with Heather and Meryl infinitely more. Nothing makes his eyes light up like seeing Evie after a day or two of absence. He's her only remaining grandparent, which is a strange thought. It's nice to see Frank so enthusiastic about spending time with her, and she knows her parents would be thrilled to see he's stepped into the role in their absence. She can't help but feel a little sympathy for Julie when Frank doesn't show her son the same commitment.

"I'm sure it hasn't been easy for Julie to become the mistress that destroyed the marriage of

Delta County's beloved Heather Green," Meryl says, which is drastically nicer than anything she's ever said about Julie in the past. "But maybe she shouldn't have slept with a married man, and she wouldn't have half the town calling her an adulterous little bitch." *There it is.*

"Hey, as I said, I'm not exactly a fan of that young lady, but it takes two to tango. The way my son acted brings me more shame than I can put into words. When I fell in love with Lisa, it was just that: love. I suffered years of mental anguish to protect her because I loved her so much. Ryan threw away the perfect family for something that doesn't even resemble love. His ability to live a double life makes me see the resemblance to his mother more than ever."

Heather knew Frank was disappointed in his son's actions, but she's never heard him speak of Ryan this way, with such hostility.

"I can't believe I'm sticking up for either of them, but it was a one-time transgression. From what they've told me, they were both incredibly intoxicated. I'm not saying it's excusable, but I don't know that I'd consider it to be living a double life, right?" Heather asks before reaching forward to crack open her can of ginger ale.

Frank doesn't respond, he only looks at her. First, with surprise, then, with sympathy.

"Heather, I'd rather do anything on earth than be the reason you ever feel another moment of pain in your life, but I'd be remiss if I say this. The idea that Ryan and Julie were a one-time transgression is laughable."

All at once, Heather sees herself the way others must see her all the time. Naïve. Gullible. Foolish. Pathetic. Of course, Ryan and Julie had a full-blown affair. Of course, their child didn't result from the tragic misfortune of getting pregnant from a one-night stand. They must have laughed all the way home from counseling after telling her that whopper of a lie. They probably raised their expensive glasses of champagne that night to toast to his unbelievably stupid ex-wife.

"I'm an idiot, aren't I?" Heather barely gets the words out before she chokes back a tear.

Frank and Meryl both speak at once, leaning forward to comfort her. He smiles and motions for Meryl to go first.

"No, Heather, you try to see the good in people. That's why you didn't believe in Mitzi's evil until you heard it straight from Frank and Lisa. It's why you were so quick to forgive Kelly and thank God you did. It's why you invited me to move in the minute Rick passed. You're just a good-natured person, sweetheart."

"Counseling is supposed to be about honesty. It's supposed to help us heal through telling our truths. I can't believe they sit there in those sessions and lie to me. I just can't believe it."

Frank doesn't say another word, he just leans forward and takes Heather in his arms while she has a long, overdue cry. She cries for the loss of any resemblance to a family she's ever had. She cries for Kelly. For Dottie. For Lisa. She cries until she has nothing left. She leans back on the couch, exhausted. The sounds of Evie fussing softly sound from the baby monitor. Frank offers to go pick up some pizzas and come back. He knows nobody is in the mood to cook.

Heather glances down at her phone before answering.

"That sounds great, but would you mind ordering a little extra? Quinn Harstead is stopping by."

Chapter Twenty

"I think we need to talk," Quinn says, after helping Heather clear the last of the dinner plates and load them into the dishwasher.

Heather doesn't need to ask why.

"Sure, let me just see if Mer will watch Evie for a minute. We can light the firepit out back and have a glass of wine if you'd like?"

Quinn gives Heather a devious smile.

"I don't know, Heath. Last time I had a glass of wine in a backyard with you, you made me question whether or not my best friend killed a janitor back in 1999 and made it look like a suicide."

Heather inhales sharply to laugh and momentarily chokes before coughing until her throat settles.

"What are you two gals laughing about in here?" Meryl asks as she descends the stairs next to the kitchen. She claims nothing is going on with her and Frank, yet she never uses the downstairs bathroom when he's over. Heaven forbid he hear her urinate.

"Oh, nothing important. Hey, would you mind watching Evie for the next thirty minutes so we can have a glass of wine out back?" Heather asks, glancing into the living room as she says it. Frank is sitting on the couch and bouncing Evie on his knee. He's telling her a story and tickling her each time he finishes a sentence. She laughs every time like she doesn't see it coming. *Please stay this age forever,* Heather thinks.

"I don't think I'm getting her away from Grandpa Frank, but I'll be happy to supervise them while you girls enjoy a drink. Just promise me you'll stay here if you have more than one, Quinn."

"Yes ma'am, that's a promise," Quinn answers. She tells herself it's completely natural to ache for her mother each time an older woman shows concern for her well-being. It doesn't mean she hasn't grieved properly. Vicki would be so proud of her for coming to that conclusion on her own.

Heather reaches up into the cabinet and pulls down two plastic wine glasses; perfect for outdoor drinking because they have lids to prevent bugs from diving into her cabernet. She walks over to the pantry, slides open the door and fills both glasses from the spout of a brown box on the shelf. Quinn cackles and it startles Heather so much, she nearly drops one of the glasses.

"Damn, Heath, are times that tough? Do you need to borrow a few bucks?"

Heather looks at Quinn's line of sight, directly to the box of wine.

"You know what, Oprah? This box is only $12.99 and it's the equivalent of three bottles. It's called being a smart consumer. Look it up."

Quinn throws her head back and laughs so hard she snorts.

"You've been rich too long," Heather mumbles, handing Quinn the glass and walking past her to open the patio doors. "I have two flannel blankets out here that I purchased last month from Fleet Farm in Green Bay. I hope they are to your liking, your majesty."

"Oh, shut up," Quinn smiles, wiping tears from her eyes. "I can't wait to tell Aiden I drank wine out of a cardboard box."

Heather rolls her eyes before leaning forward to turn on the gas firepit in the center of the deck.

"So, what did you want to talk about?" she asks, keeping her attention on Quinn while also grabbing a lighter off the patio table to ignite a few citronella candles that surround them on the deck.

Quinn wraps one of the blankets tightly around her shoulders and sets her wine on the edge of the firepit.

"Heath, I can't help but feel that you're upset about *Midnight*. Yes, Malorie's life is loosely based on yours, but that's just it: loosely. I've used inspiration from people in my life for every character I've ever written. Obviously, had I known any of this was possible, I would have never used you as inspiration. You have to believe that."

Heather furrows her brow.

"So you *do* think someone is copying the book? Do you also think I have something to do with it?"

Quinn immediately starts shaking her head and pulls both hands out of the blanket to hold them up in protest.

"No, for the record, I don't. I think it's a pure coincidence that Dottie and Susan were killed around midnight. They haven't even nailed down their exact times of death and everyone is running wild with this connection. I think people just love a good conspiracy theory."

"And Malorie ended up being the killer. Does that mean you think I'm capable of killing for sport?"

Quinn looks at Heather with so much sympathy, it nearly breaks her.

"Heather. Of course not. When I was writing the character of Malorie, I decided that her backstory was going to be a well-loved, popular girl who lost her family in an accident that ended up being intentional. Those were the only similarities to you, I promise. Truth be told, the rest of Malorie's characteristics came from a girl I roomed with in college."

Heather considers this for a moment.

"I'm sorry I didn't read the book earlier. It was really, really good, Quinn."

Quinn leans forward with a smile.

"Don't feel bad, I just found out that our dear Vicki hasn't read *any* of my books."

Heather gasps and then smiles so wide; her teeth illuminate in the light of the firepit flames.

"Damnit, Vicki."

Quinn grabs her plastic wine tumbler and reaches forward to toast with Heather.

"She might not be a Quinn Harstead reader, but she sure has saved us both from the ledge a few times, my friend."

Heather clinks her glass with Quinn's.

"She sure the hell has."

Chapter Twenty-One

Shortly after Quinn leaves, it's as if the heavens opened directly above the house on Ogden Avenue and dropped every ounce of rain down, along with lightning and thunder loud enough to wake the dead.

"Well, there goes any chance of Evie sleeping through the night," Heather says after she hears her wailing through the baby monitor after a particularly loud crack from the sky.

"I just love an early fall storm," Mer says, holding her hot cup of tea a little tighter as she wiggles her socked feet in front of the fireplace. She has scooted the chair and ottoman so close, Heather is mildly concerned she's going to scorch them before the night is over.

No alcohol, no casino, musing about the storm instead of complaining; what is going on with Mer? She and Heather's Uncle Rick got together when she was an infant, but she wonders if this is what Aunt Meryl acts like when she is freshly in love. She looks back at her again as she's climbing the stairs to get Evie. Meryl is gazing outside at the rain hitting the picture window with a lazy smile. That's it; Meryl is smitten. She smiles to herself as she makes it to the top of the stairs before stopping in her tracks. She hears running water. *Did she put Evie's noise machine on the wrong setting? She always puts it on dishwasher sounds; it's her favorite.*

She hurries her pace down the hall to Evie's room and gasps when she opens the door. There is water coming from the ceiling at a steady pace and pooling on the floor. Although the leak is at the opposite end of the room as Evie's crib, Heather sprints to grab her and holds her tightly as she jogs back down the stairs to tell Meryl.

After surveying the situation, Meryl says there isn't much they can do until the morning. She puts two five-gallon pails below the leak, with a plastic tarp underneath.

"Looks like you're rooming with me tonight, sweetie," she says as she kisses Evie's soft forehead. Evie smiles as if she understands.

Yet again, Heather's mind travels back to her blog and Instagram account. A leak in the roof over the nursery on a stormy night after having a drink with a bestselling author on her back deck? Her social media followers would have been hanging on every word of the Instagram posts and stories detailing her journey to find a roofer and subsequent attempts to patch the ceiling herself. Will there ever be a day she can comfortably log back on? She wonders if her once-loyal followers even know about

Evie. Of course, they do. Even though she was no longer sharing her everyday activities, the tabloids continued to do it on her behalf for months on end. The National Enquirer went as far as to suggest the baby was a result of her tryst with a guard at the jail shortly after being booked. How are they able to print these lies week after week and get away with it?

That night, she holds Evie close and barely sleeps. Between the booming thunder and anxiety over rolling on top of her sweet baby, Heather stares at the ceiling and longs for a deep slumber that never comes. The sun is shining through the curtains and Evie begins to whimper once Heather finally manages to drift off for a fleeting moment. Her first waking thought is the cost of fixing the roof and the possibility that it's been leaking for months without her knowledge and there's some sort of rot throughout her attic that she's not aware of. What if there is mold? She thinks of the summer cold Evie had and wonders if it could be some sort of sickness from the imaginary mold she is now convinced exists in her walls and ceiling. She thinks of her small savings account being wiped out by the repair bill. Inevitably, she thinks about how repair bills were never a concern when she was married to a Matthews. Sure, she had a lot of issues, but money was never among them.

Hearing the sounds of Evie waking, Meryl lightly pushes open the door to Heather's bedroom and peeks her head inside.

"Morning sleepyheads. How'd we do in here all night?"

"Not well," Heather responds and drops her head back onto the pillow.

"Well, it sounds like mommy might need a few more minutes of rest. How about baby Evie and Aunt Mer have a little breakfast and watch some cartoons?" Mer says in a cooing voice as she bends over to pick up Evie, who is reaching her small little arms out for her. "I've also got a few numbers for roofers. Want me to make some calls?"

Heather lifts her head slightly, squinting from the sun that seems entirely too bright for a fall morning in northern Michigan.

"Mer, I'd appreciate that more than you could imagine. I just need like an hour of sleep, and I'll be good as new."

Meryl smiles and lifts Evie's hand to wave goodbye to her mom as she slowly closes the door behind them. Three and a half hours later, Heather jolts awake in a panicked state, not remembering what day it is or where Evie went. She exhales, remembering she still has people who look out for her and do whatever they can to make her life a hell of a lot easier. Maybe things aren't so bad after all.

Chapter Twenty-Two

"I can't explain it. He's just been acting weird. I don't know. Maybe he's just not into me anymore."

Quinn is willing and able to report for duty as Jessie's best friend – she's been doing it for over twenty years. She's there to celebrate the good times, hold her hand through the hard times, and lend a sympathetic, listening ear for all the times in between. However, she has to draw the line when it comes to listening about the relationship woes Jessie is having…with her brother.

"Jess, I love you so much, but I can't. He's my brother and he's an idiot. We've established that."

A tear trails down Jessie's cheek and she quickly wipes it.

"You're right. I shouldn't have even brought it up."

Quinn grabs her hand.

"Don't be like that. You're my best friend. But, come on. I can't give romantic advice when it involves Matt."

Quinn is incredibly thankful for her decades-long friendship with Jessie, yet also frustrated that she doesn't have any other close girlfriends for situations like this. She used to hang out with a few girls from her company, but since she took the job working for Quinn, those friendships fizzled out. She's at Quinn's house seven or eight hours a day and the rest of her time is apparently spent with Matt.

"Hey, I've got an idea. How about you talk to Christy about it? She loves girl talk. Go, go," Quinn says, ushering Jessie out of her bedroom and closing the door behind her.

"You're an asshole, Quinn," Jessie shouts from outside the door before padding down the stairs.

"An asshole who needs to get some writing done," Quinn mumbles to herself as she hops back onto her plush mattress and opens her laptop.

She can't help herself; she googles the latest news from Delta County. This will inevitably result in thirty to forty minutes of mindless scrolling before she actually starts working on her current manuscript, but she needs to know what's going on. At the top of the search results, there is an article posted by TV6 just twenty minutes prior. Her heart sinks when she sees the headline. The autopsy results have been released for both victims. Dottie and Susan were not manually strangled. They both died as a result of ligature strangulation, most likely with a thin rope or cord.

Just like the victims in *Midnight*.

In fact, Malorie is finally caught when a spool of weathered rope is discovered in her basement by a neighbor who stops by to fix her clothes dryer. The texture is a perfect match to the wounds around the necks of all four victims in the book. This is not good. Quinn knows the whispers of a copycat committing the murders are now going to be a lot more than whispers. She vows not to check her email until she can pop a few anxiety meds.

As hard as she's tried to deny it, someone killed two women in Escanaba in the exact manner and timeframe as her bestselling novel. What are the chances? She wonders if she should call one of the officers on the case. What help could she possibly provide? Instruct them to read the fictitious book she wrote about murders in a neighboring town? This isn't a movie; they aren't going to invite her to work alongside them and catch the perp. They will probably politely thank her for her suggestion and slam the door behind her.

Quinn is startled when her bedroom door swings open and Aiden comes jogging in, fresh from his workout. He wipes the sweat from his forehead with the sleeve of his hoodie and leans down to quickly kiss Quinn on the cheek.

"How's writing?"

She gives him a grin.

"Quinn, you have a deadline!" he laughs. "I'm not letting you out of this room until you've written two chapters."

"I'm a little distracted. They just released the autopsy results for Dottie and Susan. They were both strangled with a rope, just like in my book."

Aiden leans forward and turns her laptop in his direction. He quickly scans the article.

"Babe, it says a cord or a rope. They aren't even sure. I think connecting these murders to the book is a bit of a stretch."

He continues reading, before raising his eyebrows and tapping the screen.

"Hah, it says right here. Both women had a slightly high level of doxylamine found in their system. If I remember correctly, none of the victims in *Midnight* were drugged."

How did she miss this? She'd been so focused on the cause of death, she quit reading the rest of the article. Both women had elevated levels of the active ingredient for sleeping pills in their systems, but they weren't found in either of their homes or purses. According to family and friends, neither woman was known to take any sleeping aid other than melatonin.

"Maybe the killer drugged them because they weren't strong enough to overpower them without assistance. Maybe a woman did it," Quinn says.

"Don't you dare say you suspect Heather. That woman has been through enough, Quinn."

Quinn shakes her head slowly.

"No, babe, I don't. I'm just trying to think through this."

Aiden kisses her once more and then makes his way to the master bathroom. As she hears the sound of the shower turning on, Quinn leans back on her pillows and thinks about what female would have the motive to kill both women.

Why Dottie? She was a saint. Either she had an enemy nobody is aware of, or this was the work of a truly homicidal maniac with no motive at all. Either option sends a chill down her spine.

Chapter Twenty-Three

"So, I guess I'm just not understanding why the bill is so much more than the estimate."

The roofer pulls off his Detroit Tigers hat and wipes the sweat from his brow with the back of his weathered, tanned hand.

"Ma'am, I explained the further damage I found while I was up there. I even took a few photos on my cell phone here if you'd like to see them."

Heather looks at the phone clipped to his waist. It's splattered with who-knows-what from construction sites and its screen is cracked in four different places.

"That's fine. I'm sure you're not just taking advantage of me because I'm a woman, right? My father-in-law is a lawyer, just so you know."

She hates herself before the words are even out of her mouth. She remembers the boys in college who used the old "my father is a lawyer" act to make themselves feel like somebody and they were always the worst of the worst. Heather and her friends coined a term for boys like this and it was "chatch." *That frat boy is acting like a real chatch right now.* Aside from the fact that she's threatening this poor roofer who just wants to get paid, she also referred to Frank as her father-in-law, and she must stop doing that.

She holds her hands up in apology. "Look, that came out wrong. I'm sure that the damage was bad, and you had to fix it. Money is just a little tight and I would have appreciated a heads up, that's all."

The roofer scans his eyes around the palatial living room and foyer, where they are standing. Heather reads his mind.

"I know how it looks, but no I don't come from money. It's a long story."

How is it even possible this guy doesn't know who she is?

She asks him to wait while she grabs her checkbook and meets Meryl coming in from the back deck where she was enjoying an afternoon cocktail, and although she'll later deny it, a cigarette. Heather tells her about the bill being higher than the quote.

"Ah, I don't think so. Where is the little crook?"

Heather's face reddens and she tries to stop Mer before she shakes her arm free of Heather's grip and stomps into the foyer.

Ten minutes later, after a convenient phone malfunction in which the roofer cannot actually produce photographic evidence of the damage (was there ever any? What if Heather would have accepted his offer to see it the first time?), the bill has been reduced back down to the original estimate and he is pulling out of the driveway, check and hat in hand.

"Mer, I can't thank you enough. I really didn't have an extra sixteen-hundred dollars just laying around. And what kind of contractor doesn't climb down the ladder and tell you about extra work needed before he does it?"

Meryl shakes her head and smiles.

"Oh, Heath. I've just been living as a woman a lot longer than you and have a lot shorter fuse when it comes to being taken advantage of. You'll learn."

After a few light taps on the front door to announce their arrival, it swings open, and Frank and Ryan come strolling into the house. Evie is still in her little enclosed play area on the living room floor, and she squeals when she sees them. Frank and Ryan's faces light up as they both hold their hands out to reach for her and laugh when they bump into each other.

"Guys, I'm so sorry. Time got away from me and I don't even have her ready yet. Mer and I just dealt with this jerk who tried to overcharge me for patching a leak and it's thrown my whole day off. I'll be right back," Heather says before heading upstairs to pack a few things for Evie's stay at her father's house.

By the time she trots back down the stairs, everyone is staring at her.

"What?"

Frank shakes his head in annoyance.

"Kent Savard? You hired Kent Savard to fix your roof? That idiot has so many judgments against him, I doubt he even still has a valid contractor's license!"

Heather's heart drops. "How would I have known that? I don't regularly keep up with roofers around here! I've never needed one!"

"Heath, remember he took that little old lady for half her savings account and didn't even do the work? We watched the story on channel 6 and you cried and asked if we could send her money," Ryan adds, holding Evie and bouncing slightly to keep her content.

"That's him?" Heather gasps. "Also, did we ever send her money?"

Ryan smiles. "No, you looked up the online fundraiser and saw that the goal had already been met. You cried again at how supportive our community is." Heather smiles at the memory before remembering that she's silently furious with Ryan for lying to her about Julie once again. Unfortunately, she promised Frank she'd get it out of him on her own, without throwing him under the bus and she's a woman of her word.

"Why isn't this scumbag in jail?" Meryl asks. Her foot is tapping, and Heather knows this is a sure sign she's about to explode.

"The judgments are all civil cases. I believe he's done a little time for unrelated offenses, but he keeps getting released and women like you keep hiring him," Frank smiles.

Heather hands Frank Evie's bag and walks over to Meryl. "The important thing here is that you talked him down on price and he'll never be in our home again."

"Well, there's rain in the forecast tonight. I'll be waiting to hear if the leak was actually fixed," Frank says. "I have a sneaking suspicion it wasn't."

The thought infuriates Heather. That was a very sizeable check she just wrote him. She had to transfer money from her savings account, something she tries hard not to do. It will take months for her to replace that money. Hell, maybe longer if she doesn't accept the bookstore position.

"Anyway, changing the subject. We're going to go pick out some pumpkins and I'll be sure to take plenty of pictures because I already know you're going to ask," Ryan says before kissing Evie on the forehead. She giggles and holds both of her hands to Ryan's face before mumbling.

"You're going to the pumpkin patch? Her first time and I'm not going to be there?"

Heather feels like she could pass out cold, right there on the floor. Fall is her favorite season. With everything going on, she barely registered that the fridge calendar says October. It's going by so fast. She normally has all her Halloween decorations up by the first of her favorite month.

"Would you like to come with us?" Ryan asks, with an arrogant smile. Of course, she doesn't want to. Julie and their illegitimate child will no doubt be in attendance. Julie has stolen so much from her already. She can't believe Evie's first time at the pumpkin patch won't be with her own mother.

"Heath, you and I will take her later in the week. She's a baby, she'll never remember that she's already been. You can take all the pictures you want; I promise I won't complain," Meryl offers.

Frank clears his throat.

"Nobody says co-parenting is easy, but I've seen a lot of messy divorces and custody battles and you two are handling it better than anyone I know.

There are going to be plenty of bittersweet occasions like this, but you kids can handle it. I'm sure of it. And Mer is right, Evie will never remember, and it will seem brand new to her next week."

"Thanks, Frank," Heather says, forcing a smile.

She kisses her daughter goodbye, just as she does every single week, and mixes herself a strong cocktail before retrieving her Halloween decorations out of the storage area in the garage. Meryl agrees to help after Heather mixes her a drink as well.

For the next three hours, the women hang orange string lights, stretch fake cobwebs over the bushes in front of the house, and strategically place spooky décor throughout their beautiful home. She turns off her Spotify Halloween playlist after *Monster Mash* begins to play for the third time. They both collapse on the couch, exhausted but proud of their work. The house is tastefully decorated and very closely resembles the "October Décor" board Heather compiled on Pinterest when she and Ryan purchased the home. She once again mentally acknowledges how much her followers would love to see the giant home on Ogden Avenue all decked out for the holiday.

No sooner than they kick their feet up on the couch, a crack of thunder startles them both and it's only seconds before raindrops begin hitting the roof. Neither wants to say it out loud, but they are both remembering Frank's words from earlier about how the shady roofer probably didn't even fix the leak. They sit in silence for an eternity before standing and slowly walking up the stairs.

Heather enters Evie's room first, with Meryl directly behind her, and she flips the light switch on. Both of their eyes travel to the pool of water on the carpet, being fed by a steady drip from the ceiling.

"That worthless little shit," Meryl mumbles.

Chapter Twenty-Four

"What's the appropriate outfit for a double date with my *brother*?"

Aiden grabs Quinn by the waist and pulls her back. She doesn't want to laugh, but she can't help it as she squirms away from his grip.

"How about you just chill and consider this a dinner with Matt and Jessie, something we've done a hundred times?"

Quinn cocks her head to the side, her standard response when Aiden is being too rational.

"She's just been trying to vent to me a lot about him lately and I'm not trying to be in the middle of my brother's relationship issues. I have enough issues of my own," Quinn says.

Aiden smiles. "Oh, do you now?"

"Aiden! Two women have been murdered and there's a good chance the killer got the idea from one of my books. In fact, some idiots are saying I did it myself. I'd call that an issue."

Although she makes her living with words, she can never find the right ones to describe how it makes her feel when he smiles the way he's smiling at her now. Her body is transported to 1997 when her awkward teenage self laid eyes on Aiden for the very first time. She felt a way she didn't know possible, and her life was never the same. She remembers the way she yearned for him during the winter when she was months away from being able to see him again. Sometimes when he smiles at her now and looks directly into her eyes, she remembers it all. The unbearable ache of losing him and the relief in her heart of finding him again, after all the tragedy. Aiden is the best thing that has ever happened to her, and she can't believe she's still keeping Jessie's secret from him. Although she's being deceptive, she reminds herself of all the hurt it would cause if Aiden knew the truth behind his cousin's death. Quinn knows that Aiden doesn't harbor any animosity toward Sarah, whom he thinks was present during the deaths. He only blames Cassie, Vinny's true killer. If Jessie is telling the truth, Aiden's blame lies with the right person and Quinn sees no point in changing that. Cassie killed his cousin, not Jessie.

"If you're thinking of backing out of this dinner, just remember the butter flight," Aiden says as he brushes a stray hair out of her eyes.

Quinn's eyes light up.

"The butter flight," she says slowly, nodding. It's her very favorite thing about tonight's restaurant, The Freshwater Tavern. Aside from the benefit of wall-to-wall windows overlooking Lake Michigan, the staff also brings a complimentary butter flight with the breadbasket before each meal. She's not sure exactly what they put in the assorted kinds of butter or how they make them so soft, but she's always left thinking about that flight for days each time they dine there.

Quinn keeps her thoughts on the butter as Matt pulls out Jessie's chair at the restaurant; something she's never seen him do in his life. She's still thinking of the butter as she follows the sight of his arm reaching over under the table, quite obviously on Jessie's leg. She certainly continues to think of only the butter when Matt asks Jessie to move in with him, right there at the dinner table with his little sister.

"I'm sorry I've been a little off lately, I just found the perfect house for us downtown and the bank was giving me a hard time about getting the loan. Dad helped me find a new lender and we worked everything out. The house is ours," Matt beams as he tells Jessie.

"Trouble getting a loan? Why didn't you call me?" Quinn asks, wide-eyed.

"Maybe I didn't want your help," Matt snaps.

"So, dad went with you? Did he cosign for you or something?"

"What's it to you?"

"Oh, I don't know. I guess I'd like our father to enjoy his retirement, instead of being on the hook for a loan his son took out on a whim and has no plans on paying on time for the next thirty years. You should have just called me and left dad out of it, Matt."

For a split second, Aiden prepares to stand in defense because he's convinced that Matt is going to hit Quinn, right there in the middle of the restaurant. Once he sees Matt settle back in his chair, he puts both hands out and makes a motion for them both to keep their voices down.

"Quinn, I didn't take it out on a whim. I've been wanting to find a place for Jess and me for a while. The bank was giving me shit because I've only been at the dealership for a few months, so dad took me to his bank. It's not that big of a deal," Matt says, dipping his roll directly into the dish containing the cinnamon sugar butter, which he knows is Quinn's favorite.

"I can't wait to see it, babe," Jessie tells him, trying to break the tension between Matt and Quinn. It works. His eyes light up as he tells her about the big front porch and how it's walking distance to the beach.

"That sounds like it's by Heather's house," Quinn says with discerning eyes.

"Yeah, it's like three blocks away," Matt says nonchalantly. "Maybe now you'll actually come to visit."

"Of course, we'll visit man," Aiden tells him. "Congratulations."

Matt leans over the table and fist-bumps him.

"So glad someone is happy for me at this table."

"I'm happy for you, Matt. I swear I am. I just hate that you involved dad. I can't wait to see the place."

"And I'm happy that I finally know why you've been acting so weird lately," Jessie says, reaching under the table to squeeze Matt's hand. "I can't wait to put it behind us."

Quinn always pictured being involved when Matt went house hunting. She could give him design advice and help him pick out plants for the garden. She often daydreamed about writing a check for the house and surprising him for being such a great brother. She hasn't had that daydream in months.

Chapter Twenty-Five

Against Heather's wishes, Meryl calls Mitch Miller about the leaking roof. If it was something she should be claiming on her homeowner's insurance, Mitch would let her know.

"I wish I could tell you I wasn't familiar with the name Kent Savard, but he's pretty notorious around here, Heath," Mitch says as he surveys the damage; before his eyes travel the short distance to Evie's crib. "What a piece of shit."

"That's exactly what I said," Mer adds.

"Let's go sit on the porch and talk about it. I know the storm is causing your house some issues, but it sure is a beautiful night to listen to the rain," Mitch says to Heather.

"I'm so sick of your jovial mood lately. But, fine. I could use some fresh air."

Meryl casually puts her hands in her pockets, looking at the buckets and tarp they've set up in the room once again. "Well, as long as you's two have this under control, I might as well head out west."

Heather smiles. "Have fun, Mer. Win big."

Much like Quinn, Mitch grins ear-to-ear when Heather pours them each a glass of wine out of the box on her pantry shelf.

"That's adorable," he smiles.

"Oh, shut up," Heather grumbles, before handing him the lid for his plastic cup. "For bugs," she explains when he gives her a quizzical look.

"That's even more adorable. It's like there's a small elderly woman trapped in your body."

She clicks her lid on with a snap.

"You don't have to use it, but don't come crying to me for another glass of wine when a mosquito takes a bath in yours."

He holds both hands up in defense before snapping the lid onto his glass, which is sitting on her kitchen island.

"You know, the last time I sat out here with you was the night I found Susan's body," Heather says as she bends her head to travel under Mitch's arm while he holds open the front door.

"I know. I think about that a lot. I'm so sorry you were alone. It must have been terrifying."

Heather nods. "I've had a lot of trauma in my life, but that was a new one."

A shiver runs through her body as she takes a seat in the rocking chair. The rain is bringing the temperature down, and there is frost in the forecast for later in the week. Fall is in full gear, and it will be winter before they know it.

Mitch unzips his fleece jacket, adorned with his Miller Insurance Group logo, and wraps it around Heather's shoulders.

"Wow, it's like we are freshmen again," she says, pulling her arms through the sleeves of the jacket.

"By freshman year, you were already wearing that asshole's jacket. I never stood a chance," Mitch says.

"Don't act like you were interested in me in the slightest. You only had eyes for Kell Bell."

Mitch's hazel eyes find Heather's and lock tight. This makes the hair on the back of her neck stand on end. He waits for a beat before speaking.

"You can choose to believe me or not, but I have no reason to be untruthful to you. There was something magical about you and Kelly. You were both beautiful, smart, and talented, and you were always laughing. I think every guy in school was a little in love with you both."

Heather instinctively grabs his hand and squeezes. "That is so nice Mitch. I'm sure those boys are running for the hills now, with what a mess I turned out to be."

A concerned look fills his eyes, and he squeezes Heather's hand in return, holding it tight while he speaks again.

"Don't you ever say that about yourself, Heath. You made a decision that not many people can blame you for. You're a knockout and a wonderful mother. You're still the total package."

She tilts her head and smiles. Kindness means more to her now than ever.

"So what if you're also a felon," he adds with a wink.

She slaps his hand away and throws her head back in laughter. "I knew you were being too nice. You had to throw some little jab in there."

She stands and unzips his jacket, handing it back to him. "It's pretty cold out here, I'm just going to go grab a blanket or two so neither of us is miserable."

He begins to protest, and she ignores him, continuing her entrance into the house. She's back out moments later with a hoodie and an oversized gray blanket. She lifts the blanket to reveal the boxed wine, which she sets on the small table between them.

"You've got it all covered," Mitch says.

"This blanket is huge, if we scoot our chairs closer and kick our feet up on the footrest, we can both cover up," Heather responds, moving her chair a few inches to the right before waiting on his response.

For the next hour or so, Mitch refills their glasses several times as they rotate between silently admiring the rain and telling stories from days gone by. A few times, Mitch leans in to reach for the wine and their knees or toes briefly touch. Each time makes Heather want to reach over and embrace him. It's not even sexual energy, it's more of a yearning for companionship. A need to be held and hugged and protected. She tells herself it must be the magic combination of red wine, drizzling rain, and the orange twinkly lights lining her porch. There's no way she's becoming interested in Mitch as a partner, it's just her mind playing tricks. It's kind of like in college when she'd be three Malibu and pineapple juices deep at her favorite bar, wearing a new outfit from the mall, and swooning over some idiot who is only known by his last name and spends the excess funds from his student loans on cocaine each semester. By morning, Heather always realized she wasn't really attracted to those boys, she was just experiencing a temporary high from the liquor and new clothes. Tonight is no different.

Against her better judgment and with the aid of Bota Box Red Blend, she asks Mitch if he's been seeing anyone.

"Not anyone worth mentioning. A few dates here and there, but nobody with staying power. What about you?"

Heather laughs and dribbles a little wine down her chin before wiping it with the sleeve of her sweatshirt.

"No. The only man around here these days is Frank."

"And roofers who scam you out of your savings account," Mitch adds.

The mere mention of that stupid roofer is enough to raise Heather's blood pressure. She still cannot believe he took advantage of her like that and she's in even more disbelief that she let him. She leans back and retrieves her phone from the window ledge. "I'm texting him."

"Heath, I'm all holding this guy accountable, but you've had a bit to drink. Maybe wait until the morning?"

"Too late," she speaks in a bit of a slur, furiously tapping away on her screen before pressing send and placing the phone back on her window ledge. "I may never get my money back, but at least now he knows exactly what I think of him. I should stand up for myself more often, that felt really good."

Chapter Twenty-Six

Quinn sits straight up in bed, not quite sure where she is. Her eyes dart around the dark room, searching for something familiar. Her pulse quickens when she feels someone in the bed next to her. Relief washes over her when she sees 3:55 on the alarm clock to her right. The same alarm clock she sees every morning.

"Bad dream?" Aiden mumbles, barely stirring. "What was this one about?"

Unlike her reoccurring nightmares about being attacked in her own home or somehow ending up naked on a toilet in front of a crowd; this one she can't tell Aiden about.

"I don't remember," she whispers. "Sorry for waking you."

But she does remember. In fact, she remembers more details from this nightmare than most she's had. She was back at Camp Shady Oaks and Jessie was on a rampage. Quinn was hiding from her in one of the bunks when Jessie came bursting through the cabin door. She checked under every bunk until she threw a mattress out of her way and found Quinn hiding underneath. Just before she was attacked, Quinn could see Jessie had an accomplice. It was Matt.

Quinn is too disturbed to sleep. She keeps replaying every moment of the dream that she can remember. *What does it all mean?* She makes a mental note to ask Vicki her thoughts during their next session. She, of course, hasn't told Vicki about Jessie being the Shady Oaks Killer, so she can't exactly be honest about what may have inspired the nightmare. She's more interested in hearing Vicki's thoughts regarding why Matt was seen as a villain in her dream. Sure, she's not thrilled he's dating her best friend, but she's never feared him or felt like he was out to get her. She may have to book an extended therapy session for this one.

Aiden's alarm goes off at 6:45 and she closes her eyes, pretending she wasn't wide awake and staring at the ceiling for the last three hours.

"I'm going to get in a quick workout before my conference calls. Love you," he says, kissing the top of her head before hopping out of bed. The amount of energy this man has first thing in the morning should be outlawed. He won't even have a cup of coffee until after his workout and Quinn isn't sure how it's possible to be awake and functioning that long without caffeine.

She stares at the wall for another twenty minutes before reluctantly crawling out from under the covers and wrapping herself in an oversized robe. She closes herself in the master bathroom and immediately smells breakfast scents wafting through the vents. Randall usually only cooks full breakfasts when they are expecting company. She checks her watch, but the date isn't ringing any bells. She's sure of it; she hasn't invited anyone over this morning and it's definitely not anyone's birthday.

Curiosity gets the best of her, so she slides on her fuzzy slippers and heads downstairs. Sure enough, Randall is in the middle of cooking a full spread. Christy is sitting at the breakfast bar with a fresh latte from Quinn's new espresso machine.

"What in the hell are you doing up so early?" Quinn asks, still rubbing the sleep from her eyes.

Bruce enters the kitchen from his security office, also holding a steaming cup of something.

"And you? Am I still sleeping? What is going on?"

Christy rises from her barstool and pinches the tip of Quinn's nose, just like her father does.

"Look at the calendar, my friend."

Quinn walks to the fridge, her pointer finger traveling down the map of October until she lands on this random Saturday morning. There it is, in bold letters. Everyone's favorite day in the Harstead/Brooks household: Pumpkin French Toast Day. Randall waits until his very favorite pumpkin patch is open in the small neighboring town of Rock, handpicks pie pumpkins until he finds the perfect selection, and makes the greatest French toast of everyone's lives. It's become an unofficial holiday around here and Quinn cannot believe she forgot.

"I'll forgive you this time, boss," Randall yells from the stove. He's also cooking bacon, donuts, and homemade maple syrup, tapped from a tree on the property. Looking out the patio doors beyond the kitchen resembles the beginning of a Hallmark movie. Just past the steam rising steadily from the stove, rust-colored leaves are floating down from the trees that hang over the house and a light wind is picking up leaves from the top of the pile Bruce raked yesterday and blowing them around the yard. ESPN College Gameday is on the kitchen TV, although the first kickoff isn't for hours. Christy gives Quinn a quick wink before adding pumpkin spice creamer to the coffee she is making for her. *This* is autumn in northern Michigan.

Quinn hears the chime as the front door opens and she glances at Bruce. Her head of security (well, the *only* member of security) is eating an apple cider donut and placing early bets for today's games on his laptop. He doesn't even register that someone is entering the house.

"Happy French Toast Day!" Jim yells as he removes his craggy newsboy cap and throws it on the breakfast bar, nearly knocking over Quinn's coffee.

"Your dear daughter nearly forgot about it," Christy says, raising her eyebrows as if she just delivered a piece of juicy gossip.

Jim puts his hand on his chest and staggers backward, feigning a heart attack. "Say it isn't so, baby," he says to Quinn, holding both his hands together in prayer. Quinn rolls her eyes and hugs him.

"I've got a lot on my mind, dad," she says.

"Living in a mansion and having this handsome devil for a father starting to get to you, my dear?" he asks, kissing the top of her head.

"Well, I've got a deadline for my new book and my last book is inspiring murders in my hometown, so yes. I've got a lot on my mind."

He puts both hands on her shoulders, leans forward, and places his forehead directly on hers. "Sweetheart, I know. I'm sorry. Your dear dad was just trying to make a joke."

"It's just been weird, dad. It's been a weird, weird month."

"I'd love to hear more about it, toots, but Randall is setting the table and I can't let that damn Christy stick me with the ugly pieces of French toast like she did last year."

Christy sticks out her tongue at Quinn's dad before smiling and wrapping her arm through his. "I'll share the freshest pieces with you this year, Jim. Come on."

"Pumpkin French Toast Day!" Aiden yells, running down the stairs, fresh from a shower. "I purposely scheduled an hour before my meetings begin so I could give this meal the time it deserves."

"I'm honored you penciled me in, Mr. Brooks," Randall says with a bow. Aiden puts him in a headlock and Randall pushes him off, straightening his hair when he is released. "What did I tell you about touching my hair?"

"That I should do it often, and early in the morning?" Aiden says with a smile. Randall rolls his eyes and walks back to the kitchen for the rest of the food. Just as he reenters the dining room and sets the last two serving plates on the table, the front door flies open, and Jessie and Matt come running in.

"We aren't too late, are we?" Jessie says breathlessly.

"Not at all," Quinn smiles, pulling out the chair next to her.

"Thank God," Matt grumbles before pulling out his chair.

"I thought you said basic white girls with too much time on their hands and nothing in their basic little heads were the only ones who got excited about pumpkin-flavored food?" Quinn asks Matt.

"Yeah, well. That's before I found out how fucking good this French toast is."

"Language," says Christy.

"But you let Quinn and dad swear in here all the time," Matt protests.

Christy, per usual, is no-nonsense.

"That's because your sister signs my paycheck and your dad is my future ex-husband."

Jim gasps. Nobody has ever used his line back on him. "You're damn right," he smiles, before taking a stack of French toast for his plate.

"I'm surprised you're not all glued to the local news," Matt says before grabbing entirely too many pieces of bacon and shoving two in his mouth at the same time.

"It's game day, why would we need to watch the local news?" Bruce asks.

Matt looks around the table at everyone, their eyes locked in on him, eagerly awaiting a response.

"You guys didn't hear? The strangler struck again."

Chapter Twenty-Seven

The fact that Heather and Ryan are still going through with their appointment with Vicki today, despite Julie being bedridden with the flu, is like some sort of alternate universe where they sought couple's counseling before it was too late. Watching Ryan spew lie after lie tells Heather it would have always been too late.

She hasn't confronted him about the truth yet. The one Frank confessed with pain in his eyes. He and Julie had an affair, right under Heather's nose, for who knows how long and continue to lie about it. She wonders if Vicki knows. Is she obligated to intervene if she watches them lie to Heather, right there in her office? Was this part of her oath?

Heather has had two custody hand-offs with Ryan since she found out the truth. Both times she impressed herself with how calm and cordial she was.

For once in her life, she's keeping this information in her back pocket and holding it for a time of her choosing.

"It bothers me that Frank spends so much time with Heather and Meryl," Ryan says, his infliction indication that this grievance is part of a list he's ready to unload.

"Heather, Meryl, and Evie, you mean," Heather interrupts. "Evie, you know, his only granddaughter."

"See?" Ryan looks at Vicki. "She takes anything I say and finds a way to make me look insensitive."

Before Vicki can respond, Heather leans forward and pats Ryan condescendingly on the leg. "I'm sorry, Ryan. Please continue and explain how horrible it is that Frank is spending time with his granddaughter. I shouldn't have interrupted."

Ryan crosses his arms and leans back into the brown, overstuffed couch with a huff. Heather is sure she will begin to see this behavior from Evie in the coming years. You know, a toddler's behavior.

"Why don't I pour you both a cup of tea and let's take some deep breaths and do a reset?" Vicki asks, her voice irritatingly calm.

Heather and Ryan sit in silence while Vicki retrieves two hot cups of chamomile from her coffee bar area in the corner of her office. Heather remembers the room she used to meet with Vicki in, the cold, sterile, impersonal room in the Delta County Jail. The same room in which she met with her lawyer several times a week before her court date. Now, she gets to sit on a plush couch with several throw pillows at her disposal to squeeze or throw or lean back on. There is a melted wax lamp in the corner with some sort of apple cinnamon scent filling the room, just barely diluted by the competing smell of the pumpkin candle lit in a jar on the table next to Vicki. There are boxes of Kleenex on each of the end tables and two on the coffee table between them. This always makes Heather wonder if she should be crying more when she comes to Vicki's office.

"Now, Ryan. If it's a jealousy issue and you wish you were spending more time with your father, that's something you can easily change. Simply tell him how you feel and propose more outings. If the issue you have is the fact that it's Heather he's spending time with, don't you think it's a little cruel and unfair to not want Evie's only grandparent spending time with her and the mother of your child, who has no parents left?"

Heather wants to stand and clap. Although she vows to be impartial, sometimes she's undeniably certain that Vicki is on her side. Maybe she's been cheated on and she understands what it's like to be in Heather's shoes. Maybe she also had a horrible mother-in-law. Heather has tried to research Vicki on several occasions but hasn't been able to find much other than her psychology credentials and current licensing. She once asked Vicki if she had seen a particularly funny viral video, to which Vicki replied, "I don't have any forms of social media. It's not safe or healthy for patients to have access to my personal life on that level." Heather never asked about it again.

"You're right. I guess I just wish he wanted to spend time with Julie and Hunter, as well. It would be great to come home and find my dad there, playing with Hunter. Teaching him how to play catch. Or fish. Or anything, really. He just doesn't spend as much time with Hunter."

Vicki nods and writes this down.

"Is it possible Hunter reminds him of a turbulent time in his life? It may be similar to the reason Heather does not wish to spend time with your son."

"No offense to the kid, but I just don't feel like being reminded of my husband's infidelity each time I look at him, so I don't," Heather says calmly, blowing on her tea before taking an apprehensive sip. She shakes her head and sets the cup back on its marble coaster. Still too hot.

"There it is again, 'my husband's infidelity', I thought we were trying to move on? Isn't that why we're here?" Ryan asks.

Heather turns her head and locks eyes with him, eyes that are cold and careless. She cannot reconcile that this is the same man she once loved like there was nobody else on earth. The same person that talked Frank into driving him to Chicago so he could purchase a simple silver necklace from the Tiffany & Co. store for Heather's sixteenth birthday because he couldn't wait to see her eyes light up at that little blue box she always saw in the movies. The same man who believed in her so much, he drove to her college each weekend to study with her and help increase her GPA so she could graduate on time. The same man who proposed to her when she did graduate and promised to love her each and every day for the rest of their lives. *How.* How is this the same man?

176

Heather is done hiding what she now knows to be the truth.

"Ryan, moving on means telling the truth, no matter how hard it is. So, why don't we try doing that and we can see if I move on just a little easier?" she asks.

He shrugs his shoulders and squints his eyes, looking at Vicki rather than Heather, which infuriates her. He looks cocky. Arrogant. Far too superior to be bothered with this line of questioning from his ex-wife.

"No, don't look at Vicki. Look at me. Tell me the truth about you and Julie."

"What are you going on about? I've told you. Dozens of times. In this very office."

Heather takes another sip of her tea, this time she keeps tipping the mug back, letting the hot liquid coat her throat, burning a little on the way down.

"Ryan, not only are you insulting my intelligence, but you're wasting Vicki's time. Tell us both how long you were sneaking around with Julie before she got pregnant. How many times?" Heather asks. She doesn't cross her arms, she doesn't fidget. She asks with conviction before leaning back and watching him squirm.

His eyes dart from Heather to Vicki and back to Heather. She can read his mind. He's not sure how much she knows. He's preparing his lies. She cannot believe this is the man she wasted half her life with. He also takes a drink from his mug in an attempt to delay the inevitable. He stares forward for a beat before exhaling.

"I'm not sure how many," he says quietly.

Heather sees Vicki's eyes grow bigger. He had her fooled, as well. Vicki holds one hand up slightly, in Heather's direction, asking her to sit back and let the professional handle this.

"Ryan, I know this is tough, but it's important that you're truthful at this moment. When did your affair with Julie begin?"

She sees Heather staring at the pen in her hand and she sets it down on her notebook, moving both to the table next to her. She clasps her hands together and leans forward, giving Ryan her full attention.

"High school," he responds.

Heather gasps. Vicki once again motions for her to sit back.

"And when did it start up again?" Vicki asks.

Ryan turns his head to Heather, before quickly turning away. He stares at the ground for a minute before his eyes meet Vicki's.

"It never stopped."

Chapter Twenty-Eight

Heather can't begin to explain why, but she calls Cindy Sanders when she gets in the car, her voice shaking as she says *"call Cindy"* to the Bluetooth system in her car. Cindy, mother of Marc, Julie's ex-husband. The husband she was apparently cheating on for the entirety of their relationship.

"I was just thinking about you!" Cindy chirps.

Despite her best efforts, Heather begins to sob. This opens the floodgates. She is crying so furiously; she can barely speak.

"Heath, deep breaths. Tell me what happened. Is the baby okay?"

Heather pops open her glove box and pulls out a handful of fast-food napkins to wipe her face. The brown, rough textured budget napkins seem to only increase the redness of her skin. She exhales and begins to laugh at the absurdity of it all. She really thought her life was going to get back to normal.

"Yes, sorry. I don't really know what happened there. Evie is great; she's with Meryl at the house and Ryan will pick her up this afternoon for his days."

After a moment of hesitation, Cindy says, "Want to grab a glass of wine at Leigh's and get a little day drunk? The winery is within walking distance for us both and they open in five minutes. You can tell me all about whatever unfortunate bastard is making you upset."

"There is nothing in life I'd rather do. Let me call Mer and make sure she's okay to watch Evie until Ryan gets there. I'll meet you there. Oh, and Cindy?"

"Yes?"

"Thank you. Thank you for knowing just what I needed."

Heather's voice is significantly calmer when she says *"call Mer"* as soon as they hang up. She's thankful for the hands-free feature, as her fingers are still trembling from the news.

Leigh's Garden Winery is one of the few places where Heather feels comfortable going after her release. Tony, the owner, has been a fervent supporter of hers and she's fairly sure he would forcibly remove anyone who gave her a hard time in his establishment. She no longer needs to ask; he's told her repeatedly that she can park in the rear alley and enter through the back door. The winery is dimly lit and there's a back room he can close off for her when she needs extra privacy, on a day like today. In short, Heather will give Tony her business as often as possible. If she still had her Instagram account,

180

she'd promote his winery free of charge. As she pulls into her special parking spot, she's suddenly ashamed, remembering the budget box she's been drinking from at home.

When she arrives through the back door, Cindy is already seated in the back room with a bottle of Mary Terry Rosé on the table with two glasses. The wine is named after Mary Terry, the woman who died in (and debatably haunts) the lighthouse where Heather found Susan's strangled body just weeks ago. Cindy holds up the bottle and winks, which makes Heather shake her head and laugh so lightheartedly, she momentarily forgets what just happened in therapy. There are very few people in Heather's life who have a morbid sense of humor like Cindy, which makes her treasure the woman even more. Tony appears from behind the bar and gives Heather a cordial embrace.

"How you holding up, kid?"

"I'm hanging in there, Tony. Thanks for giving us the back room."

"Anything for you, you know that. Also, Cindy bought enough wine from me last year to pay for my family's Christmas vacation, so you's two broads can have whatever the hell you want around here."

Cindy has now poured herself a glass and raises it in Tony's direction. "Wait until election year, I might buy enough to fund your kid's college education."

Tony laughs and pulls a purple velvet curtain closed behind him, giving the women total privacy. There are several recessed lights turned on the lowest setting and half a dozen candles are flickering throughout the room. Heather looks at the piano in the corner of the room before taking her seat.

When she and Ryan first purchased the house on Ogden Avenue, they used to walk to the winery on Friday nights to watch her high school friend Travis play old Frank Sinatra tunes for hours. She remembers the lighting and music being the perfect combination to feel pure magic once she'd had a full glass of wine. She was ridiculously grateful to be back in her hometown and all was right in the world. She wonders now if, while she was transfixed with all the wonderful things around her in this room, Ryan was thinking of Julie. She has retained very few positive memories of him after all that has happened, and now even those are tainted.

Cindy leans forward and gives Heather a heavy pour of Rosé.

"Talk to me, sweetheart."

She can't help but remember the day she sat at Ludington Grill with Cindy and poured her heart out after Mitzi gifted Julie that damn rocking horse. She's overwhelmed with the thought of how much has happened since that day.

"Well, Cin, in a way this also affects you."

This gets Cindy's attention. She sets her wine glass down and breathes deeply in preparation for what bombs Heather is about to drop.

"Today, in therapy, Ryan admitted that he began sleeping with Julie behind my back in high school. When our therapist asked him how long it was before he started seeing her again, he said he never stopped."

Cindy's chin drops like a bouncing ball and her eyes grow wide.

"So, she was cheating on my son the entire time?"

"Afraid so," Heather says with a nod.

Cindy erupts in laughter so brash; it startles Heather to her core. It's a maniacal laugh. She sounds unhinged. She stands and grabs a napkin from a server station in the corner to wipe her tears.

"That little tramp," Cindy says quietly.

"Well, it takes two, I'm afraid," Heather responds.

"I heard a few months ago that she told people my son *hit* her when he found out about the affair. He's no angel, we both know this, but he wouldn't hit a woman if his life depended on it. He had to physically stop me from driving to her house to confront her."

"How are you so sure he didn't hit her?" Heather asks, with a hint of hesitation. She doesn't want Cindy to think she's questioning her judgment, but she watched Julie sob in therapy as she detailed Marc's abuse.

"Because I was there."

Heather puts her hand on her chest in shock.

"You were there?" she asks, her eyes open wide.

"Heather, we had asked him since Hunter was born if he was sure he was the father. We all saw the resemblance and he just told us it was an unfortunate coincidence that his baby had a dimple in the same place as Ryan Matthews."

Heather flinches. She still cannot believe nobody told her. She then puts herself in their shoes and sees how uncomfortable and out of line it would be to ask someone if they knew a former rival's new baby bared a striking resemblance to their husband.

"Julie came to my house that morning. Marc had stopped by to discuss some things and she sat at that table, looked us in the eyes, and told us Ryan forced her into the sexual encounter that resulted in her pregnancy. Marc was heartbroken. He was enraged. He wanted to kill Ryan. Julie begged him to calm down and told us she was headed to Mitzi's house to confront her. She said Mitzi knew."

"She said Ryan assaulted her and his mother knew about it?" Heather asks incredulously.

"Yes, she said Mitzi told her that they were both intoxicated, and it must have been a misunderstanding. It was nothing to ruin her son's life over. Julie lived with that for months and she said the anger had finally built enough, she wanted to confront her."

"But she testified in court that the reason she was at Mitzi's house that day was to confront her about the rocking horse she gave me," Heather says.

"She also claims the man she'd been having an affair with for over a decade randomly assaulted her, instead of admitting to the affair. All I can do is laugh. Laugh so I don't strangle the little bitch. She looked me in the eyes and said he assaulted her, and I believed her. We both did."

Heather shakes her head and stares at the glass in front of her. She swirls the light pink liquid so furiously, it nearly spills over the edge.

"So, she lied to everyone about having an affair with Ryan. She lied about why she was going to Mitzi's. She lied about Ryan assaulting her. She lied about Marc abusing her. What else is this woman capable of?"

Her very next thought, of course, is that this is the woman who cares for her child two days a week. The only reason she's not with Evie now is that she has the flu if that's even truthful. Ryan has Evie and Hunter out at Frank's place on the lake so Julie can rest.

"So, what do we do?" Heather asks.

"Well, the first thing I'm going to do is tell my son. He might just have a breakdown and laugh himself silly like I just did. Then, if you want to formulate a plan to confront her, you know I'm ready and willing, my friend."

Tony slides in through the opening in the curtain and holds a hand up in apology.

"I don't want to interrupt you ladies, but I'm heading out for the day, and I just wanted to check and make sure you didn't need anything."

"We have everything we need right here," Cindy says, holding up the half-full bottle of wine.

"I'm glad to see you out and about, Heath. I'm sure it's been a long day."

Confusion washes over her. How could he know about what happened with Ryan at therapy? Was he eavesdropping on the women just now?

"Long day?" Heather asks.

"I heard they'd probably bring you in for questioning. This whole situation is so messed up and we all know you have nothing to do with what's going on. For the record, I don't think Quinn does, either."

"Oh, about Dottie and Susan? Yes, of course, they came over and asked me some questions. They know I'd never hurt Dottie. Susan, on the other hand…let's just say it's a good thing there was footage of me on the opposite end of the park."

She smiles and winks at Cindy. Cindy winks back. They both look back up at Tony.

"Oh…I'm talking about Kent Savard."

"That bastard? Oh, Cindy, I didn't even get a chance to tell you about what that jerk did to me. We might need to add him to our list," Heather says with a smile.

Tony turns white.

"Oh, Heath. Oh my god. Okay, well, has nobody called you?"

"Called me?"

"Kent Savard's body was found early this morning."

The room spins. Heather can't breathe. This isn't possible. She remembers the last text she sent him. *If you don't take care of this roof, I will see that someone takes care of you. If you know what I mean.* She added that last part because she was a little drunk and wanted to sound like a mobster. She stopped short of telling him he'd be swimming with the fishes.

"How did he die?" Heather asks, but of course, she knows the answer.

"Nothing has been released, but I was at Rosie's Diner this morning when Bob Trull got a call from his brother, who works on the force. He said he was strangled and dumped by the marina."

Heather instinctively reaches for her phone, which is still on silent from the therapy session.

It's been in her purse since she left the house this morning for her appointment.

She has fourteen missed calls, six of them from Officer Dave Simpkins.

Chapter Twenty-Nine

Thank God for modern technology. Between the outdoor security camera footage of Heather falling asleep with a book in her lap on the back deck and then the time-stamped camera footage from Evie's nursery of Heather groggily checking on her and falling asleep again in her favorite chair in the corner until daylight began to shine through the windows, there is zero chance she had time to leave the house and murder Kent Savard. They don't have his exact time of death narrowed down yet, but once again — it appears to have happened sometime in the night and Heather is certain that time will be determined to have happened around midnight like the others.

She also got an oil change at her normal spot yesterday, which logs the miles at the time of service. She drove straight home after and could account for the miles to Vicki's office and Leigh's Winery the next morning, which meant her vehicle was not driven anywhere else in the last 24 hours. This didn't seem to interest either of the detectives interviewing Heather, which made her feel that they knew she wasn't responsible.

She also volunteered the information about texting Kent late at night and even offered her phone to the men. She knew it was better to be forthright out of the gate than be caught omitting information later.

"Who knew about your disagreement with Mr. Savard?" asked one of the detectives, a new transplant to the area. Heather wondered if he was brought in because of the string of murders, but she didn't want to ask. The city of Escanaba doesn't exactly have experienced homicide detectives at its disposal, so it would make a lot of sense for the town to request backup from a bigger city downstate. She focuses on his weathered hands as he speaks and questions why a detective would have the hands of a laborer. Maybe his wife gives him a mountain of honey-do's on the weekends and he simply has the hands to show for it.

"Well, a lot of people, actually," Heather answered, suddenly ashamed of her big mouth. Since being burned by the roofer, she has vented to just about everyone she encountered. Her disdain for Kent Savard was no secret.

"Can I also mention that this man had quite a few cases against him? One was even featured on the local news. I assure you, I'm not the only woman he has screwed over."

The detective tapped his fingers a few times on the desk in front of him and then ran them over his mustache a few times, smoothing it down. Heather knew this man was stressed, even before he started fidgeting.

"Ms. Green, let me make it clear to you that I don't view you as a suspect, nor have you been officially listed as one. However, my job is to find out why the people around you keep being met with untimely deaths."

Against her better judgment, Heather asks if either detective has read Quinn Harstead's book. The book that has been the talk of the town since Dottie's body was discovered, but with these men debatably being brought in from another county, she wasn't sure if they'd know. Mustache looks over at his partner, who has barely said a word throughout the interview, and nods.

"I haven't had a chance to read Ms. Harstead's novel, but I've been given the cliff notes. Let me ask you, do you have any reason to believe someone is copying the murders in the book?" he asks.

"Someone would have to *really* despise me to frame me for murder. Unfortunately, or fortunately, I guess, the only person who I knew to hate me that much was Susan Grant. And she's dead, as we know," Heather responds. She nearly jokes that maybe they should check Julie's alibi, but these men don't seem the type to joke in the interrogation room.

They wind up the interview just as Heather has seen in countless TV shows and movies: the detective hands her a business card and asks her to call if she remembers any details they haven't already discussed. She stops herself from laughing when he says, "Remember, no detail is too small to mention. You never know how much it could help." Yes, the same line she has heard Benson and Stabler mutter a thousand times on *Law and Order: SVU*.

When Heather walks out the back door of the police station, she's startled to see Mitch Miller leaning on her vehicle. He's pressed flat against the driver's side door, staring down at his phone.

"Mitchell," she says, and he jerks his head up and slides the phone into his back pocket.

"Only my mother calls me that," he smiles. "I just heard the news, so I came here to make sure you're okay."

"I told them everything I knew, and I feel like they believed me, but I still can't grasp that this is happening."

Mitch asks if she wants to grab a cup of coffee and discuss everything, but before she can answer, a Tesla pulls into the parking lot and parks next to her vehicle. Frank and Doug Angeli, her lawyer, exit the vehicle and rush to her side.

"Why didn't you call me?" Doug demands.

"Why would I call you? I'm not in custody."

"Heather, I've told you a million times. Don't ever answer questions in a police station without me present."

Heather holds both hands up in defense and shakes her head.

"Doug, chill, I'm not a suspect. They actually wanted my help to find out why someone would be trying to frame me."

Doug gives a sarcastic laugh.

"Oh, did they?"

"Guys, I have an airtight alibi. There is no way I was anywhere near Kent Savard when he was killed. I don't need a lawyer."

Frank intervenes, attempting to diffuse the situation.

"Look, Heath, I know you're annoyed with us, but you need to remember all the cases we've worked on where a suspect dug themselves in a pretty deep hole with the words they said to a detective before we were called. In nearly every case, the client tells us that they were just trying to help and felt that they didn't say anything incriminating to the cops. We are just trying to prevent that from happening to you. Lord knows you don't need any more trouble."

Heather softens a little at this. Frank is right.

"I'm sorry, Doug, I didn't mean to have an attitude with you. It's just been a strange couple of weeks. Well, a couple of years, if I'm being honest."

Doug puts his enormous hands on Heather's shoulders and apologizes as well. Before they get back into the vehicle, the two detectives who questioned Heather exit the police station and walk into the parking lot.

"That's them," Heather whispers to Doug.

"Gentlemen!" Doug yells, before hastily walking toward them and informing the men that they will no longer be questioning his client without him present.

She can't help but mouth *sorry* in their direction behind Doug's back.

She decides to take Mitch up on his offer of an afternoon coffee and they meet at Stone's Deli. Heather didn't visit the quaint coffee shop for years after her last visit with Kelly, which was hours before her death. The thought of fresh-ground Michigan Cherry coffee and a desire to create new memories in the places that evoke bittersweet ones brought her back to Stone's months after her release from jail. Now, she's able to think of the place as her favorite shop to grab a coffee and a muffin while she's out running errands and not the place she met with her best friend on their last morning together.

Despite Heather's protests, Mitch insists on paying for their lattes and the giant cheese danish they plan to split. He begins walking to the small table in the front corner – the one that she shared with Kelly on their last visit, but she grabs his arm and leads him to a table in the back. Maybe she's convinced herself she's moved forward a little more than she has.

Mitch pulls her chair out and it makes her blush. These simple chivalrous gestures used to be commonplace, but now it's a rarity for a man to open a door or pull out a chair. It almost makes her feel like they are on a date. She scans the room to see who else is here and will be spreading the news of Heather and Mitch enjoying a cup of coffee together. Luckily, there is just one woman, who appears to be college-age. She is on her laptop with headphones in, furiously typing and scanning the open textbook next to her for reference. Heather exhales.

"Tell me how I can help," Mitch says, looking Heather in the eyes. By weight, he is literally half the man he was in high school, but his eyes remain unchanged and remind her of a simpler time in her life. She remembers his blue eyes gazing at her when he would carry her backpack off the bus or give her piggyback rides when it began to rain on a field trip. Mitch Miller has been looking out for Heather Green since she was old enough to have memories of anything at all.

"Mitch, you are doing enough. Thanks for sticking with me through all of this. I don't know what I'd do without friends like you."

He reaches over the table and squeezes her hand before cutting the pastry in half and pushing the small plate toward her.

"Heather, this guy will slip up eventually. We don't exactly have criminal masterminds around here. He's going to leave his DNA at the scene or something. We just need to lay low until that happens."

Heather's lips curl into a smirk. "I've been trying to lay low, Miller. It ain't working."

Chapter Thirty

"Babe, these candles have skulls on them. I'm not sure this is an appropriate housewarming gift."

Quinn examines the candles, placed gently in the gift basket she pieced together that morning. She thinks they pair quite well with the framed serial killer mugshots and skeleton door knocker.

"It's Matt. What did you want me to do, knit him a blanket? Give him teacups? He loves all things macabre. He'll be thrilled."

Aiden pulls Quinn in and threads his fingers through her hair softly, which is her very favorite thing.

"Babe, you do remember that Jessie has agreed to live with him in this house, right?"

Quinn looks up and kisses his chin.

"Well, I guess she better get used to the morbid death vibe if she's going to share a home with the guy, right?"

She doesn't wait for a response before turning back to the basket, fluffing the black tissue paper around her carefully curated gifts. She also included a gift card to his favorite online store, Burke & Hare Co. It's enough to buy a year's worth of skull candles once these run out. She's proud of the gift. She slips on her shoes and lifts the basket from the entryway table, balancing it on her hip as she opens the front door. Aiden takes it from her hands and rolls his eyes.

"You are a stubborn, stubborn woman. You know that, right?"

"You married me," she smiles.

After a twenty-minute drive, they pull up on the street in front of Matt's new house. Quinn is impressed; it's clean, updated, and the yard looks well taken care of. She knows he chose this house to appease Jessie; it's not his normal style. It even has a sizeable front porch, something Jessie has wanted since they drove by Heather's house on Ogden Avenue and Quinn pointed it out to her. She became fixated on having a big house with a beautiful front porch, within walking distance of the beach. Just like Heather.

"Hey, you guys made it!" Jessie yells from the front door as Quinn and Aiden exit their SUV. She's wearing a cooking apron. *She's really auditioning for the role of housewife, isn't she?* Quinn muses, before immediately scolding herself for thinking this way about her best friend.

As Quinn and Aiden walk up the steps to the front porch, she stops in her tracks. Jessie has the

196

porch situated exactly like Heather Green. Two rocking chairs with a small table on the left and a small outdoor sectional with a coffee table on the right. Jessie sees Quinn's eyes travel left and right and says, "It kind of looks like Heather's front porch, right? That's what I was going for. I wish she'd start her Instagram back up so I could have more design inspiration."

"It certainly does look just like her front porch," Quinn answers and Jessie slaps her arm lightly.

"Don't be like that, Quinn."

Quinn can never hide her feelings from Jessie; she can see right through her. It makes her wonder how she went so long before confronting her about the Shady Oaks situation. It was a hard secret to keep, so Quinn mostly avoided Jessie as often as possible.

Matt is sitting on the couch watching an old, niche horror film when they walk in the front door, which is typical behavior for him year-round, not just in October. What's not so typical is the appearance of the house. It's decorated in creams and whites, with a fresh bouquet on the kitchen table and what appears to be Chip and Joanna Gaines' entire line from Target displayed throughout the house.

"Well, Matt, I picked these housewarming gifts out for you, but it looks like your style has changed a little," Quinn says, setting the gift basket on the coffee table in front of Matt and looking around the room.

"Yeah, we're going a little more *modern farmhouse* with the place," Matt answers and Quinn exhales so sharply she nearly chokes. She leans forward and places the back of her hand on his forehead to check his temperature before he slaps it away in annoyance. "Get fucked," he mumbles.

"Matt is creating a man cave in the basement, I think your gifts would fit in perfectly down there," Jessie says from the kitchen, where she is pulling a tray of cookies out of the oven.

Quinn is annoyed, but it's not worth the fight. She goes straight to a door off the kitchen that she assumes to be the basement and says, "I'll just go set the basket down there, so it doesn't clash with your fancy new décor."

Jessie ignores Quinn's quip and offers Aiden a beer, which he gladly accepts before sitting on the couch next to Matt.

The basement is wide open and unfinished, which is perfect for Matt. He can put in whatever flooring and furniture he wants for his man cave. She imagines he'll be spending a lot of time down here. Right now, it's just a washer and dryer and about three dozen stacked moving boxes they have yet to unpack.

Quinn moves to the back of the room to place her gift out of the way when she sees her dad's old tackle box. She didn't realize he had given it to Matt. She has fond memories of him taking them out on the Escanaba River in his small fishing boat when she and Matt were children. He always kept her favorite candy in the tackle box to bribe her when she started to get antsy and begged to go home. Quinn unclasps the tackle box and opens its lid. She smiles when she sees the Swedish Pimple, a fishing lure patented by a local man decades ago. Her hands stop when she lifts the top tray and sees a rolled up section of thin rope, almost twine-like. It is exactly like the scene in her book when the neighbor is in Malorie's basement and finds the rope she used to strangle her victims. Quinn shivers and drops the spool. She knows it's not a murder weapon, it looks like it hasn't been touched in years. She had to knock the dust off the tackle box before she even opened it. She's also 99% sure that her brother would never hurt anyone, and Jessie wouldn't unless it was in defense or retaliation, like what happened at Shady Oaks.

But the thing about being 99% sure about something is that nagging little 1%.

That 1% will eat you alive.

Chapter Thirty-One

Heather Green has once again become a reluctant recluse. It began with a call from a local who considers herself an investigative journalist but couldn't uncover the truth if it bit her in the ass. It escalated with the re-emergence of gawkers outside her home, and it finally reached a fever pitch when People Magazine called her for comment (she declined) before running a story on the current drama surrounding the "Mother-in-law Murderer." She understands that this nation has a morbid curiosity when it comes to murder and magazines are just trying to sell copies, but she wishes they'd wait until everyone had some answers before shining a national spotlight on her little town once again.

She peers through a gap in her closed blinds to stare at the big pile of leaves she raked the previous week for Evie to play in. Now she's afraid to play outside with her own daughter. Meryl has stopped going to the casino, due to the nosy gamblers who insist on claiming the slot machine next to her and peg her with questions surrounding the deaths and her niece's possible involvement.

All of the SHARKs, and everyone else in her life for that matter, keep insisting to Heather that nobody *actually* believes she is capable of these crimes, the public is simply intrigued that all the victims are connected to her. Despite this insistence, none of them seem to be able to take a few days off work to spend with her while she locks herself away. They are all suddenly *swamped* at their jobs and can't make the drive. Even Rebecca, who lives in town, hasn't been by.

The two people who haven't left Heather's side (besides Meryl, who has no choice) are Mitch and Frank. They both are over often, help care for Evie, and usually bring food. Truth be told, she's gotten used to having Mitch around a little more than she cares to admit. He's so good with Evie; he even volunteered to watch her the other day so Heather could take a bath and a nap — two things that don't get to happen very often when you have a child under the age of one.

Next week is Halloween, and Heather is devastated that she won't be able to take Evie trick-or-treating. She's letting Ryan take her, as long as he promises to keep her costume over her face while in front of others. She doesn't need her innocent daughter being targeted over this nonsense.

When she's not putting on a brave face for Evie, she cries in her room, holding a pillow to her face to muffle the sounds so Meryl doesn't hear. She doesn't watch TV, as she knows exactly what every local station is discussing. She prays to a god she's not quite sure she still believes in and begs for the murderer to be found quickly. She promises not to ask for anything else as long as she lives. Well, maybe for Evie to have a happy, healthy life. But nothing else. She swears.

There's a knock at the door as she microwaves her Lean Cuisine and Heather rolls her eyes at the thought of answering it. Anyone she wants to see right now knows her well enough to just walk in, especially with all the reporters outside. Whoever is knocking on the door is an unwelcome guest. She reluctantly presses cancel on the microwave and walks to the front door. She sighs in relief when she looks through the peephole.

"Vicki," Heather says as she swings open the door and swiftly closes it behind her before any of the vultures can get a good picture. "What are you doing here?"

"I thought you could use someone to talk to. Is that okay?"

Heather huffs.

"I'm not Quinn Harstead, Vicki, I can't afford house calls. I'm sorry."

Vicki gives her a tight smile.

"Well, as a matter of fact, Quinn Harstead has paid for this session. And any further sessions you require at home until this all blows over."

Heather wants to be annoyed, but she's relieved. She needs to talk to Vicki now more than ever.

After nearly two hours of intense back and forth, Heather says goodbye to Vicki and has her leave out the back door and through the gate. She pops open the microwave and tosses the room-temperature baked ziti into the trash. Just as she considers what she's going to eat in its place, Meryl comes through the sliding back patio door, having entered discreetly through the side gate herself.

"You couldn't resist the casino, could you? What did you do, put on a disguise?" Heather teases.

"Oh, I didn't go to the casino."

Heather laughs at the absurdity of Meryl ending the discussion without offering any further information. *What is going on with her?*

"Any chance you want to talk about where you were?" Heather asks with a sweet tone.

"Ah, Christ. I can't lie to ya. I was at Frank's."

Heather cocks her head.

"Mer, if you think this little flirtation between you and Frank is a secret, I have to tell you that it's the worst-kept secret in the county."

Meryl gasps. "What do you mean?"

"I don't even have the energy to tell you all the signs you've been ignoring for months. Can we just talk about what we should do about dinner?"

Meryl's cheeks redden slightly.

"Oh, so you guys already ate. Fantastic," Heather smiles. "I'll fend for myself."

Meryl walks around the kitchen island and holds both of Heather's hands, before momentarily dropping one and leaning forward to fix a strand of her hair that has fallen over her eye.

"Frank and I have been talking about you for hours. Once this blows over, we are going to get back to normal around here. I promise you, sweetie."

"Everyone keeps using that phrase 'once this blows over,' like it's a rumor being spread that I kissed some boy in the school gym. It's not that easy, Meryl. Three people have died, they are all connected to me, and it appears that the police don't have any credible leads. What if more people die?" Heather says, tapping her foot furiously to distract her from crying. "And then what?"

Meryl inhales sharply. "Well, Heather, that's why we installed more cameras inside the house. You're going to suck it up and stay here until this *does* blow over, which it will, and heaven forbid there are any more murders, there will be no possible way for you to be a suspect. We will have footage to prove you were here."

"I can't believe I have to do this. I'm a prisoner in my own home. I thought my time being locked up was behind me."

Meryl hugs her and Heather knows it's because she's not quite sure what else to say at the moment. Heather's phone buzzes in her pocket and she looks down to see it's from Mitch. He wants to know if she's hungry. Against her better judgment, she smiles.

Chapter Thirty-Two

"I don't know how you did this before you had a publicist. I'm exhausted."

Quinn laughs. "Well, before I had a publicist, I didn't have some maniac copying one of my suspense novels in a town that normally sees one murder per century."

Jessie types a few more words on her laptop, closes it, and spins around in her office chair to face Quinn. "Okay, I've sent a standard response about how terrible you feel that someone may be imitating scenes from your *New York Times Bestselling Novel.* I replied to all 68 outlets that requested a comment. I did, however, tell Craig and Kevin that you'd call into Friday morning's show and talk to them for two to three minutes."

This makes Quinn smile. She loves Craig and Kevin's Friday morning radio show, and they are the only two people who can get an interview out of her at a time like this. She also knows they aren't going to ask any uncomfortable questions and will let her speak for herself.

"Fine," she says, glancing up at the ceiling, but Jessie knows it won't be an issue.

"So, since I've had to go into PR overdrive these last few days, any chance I can vent to you for two seconds?" Jessie asks sweetly, placing her hands under her chin in an innocent child's pose.

Quinn rolls her eyes. "Look, I'm timing you on my phone; you've got five minutes if this is about my brother. Go."

"Okay, so first he was acting distant. But then I found out it was because he was trying to buy my dream home for us to live in and the bank was giving him problems, so I understood. But now…he's acting weird again. What do you think it could be?"

Quinn momentarily considers telling Jessie it's because she took a death metal and slasher movie-loving weirdo and locked him into a modern farmhouse nightmare where he has to make the mortgage payments but decides against it.

"Well, he's been divorced less than a year. Maybe he's just panicking about getting back into a serious relationship so soon."

Jessie looks incredibly hurt as if this is a possibility she hadn't yet considered.

"Quinn, will you please talk to him? I can't stand this. I don't care how bad the news is; I want to hear it."

She wants Quinn to talk to her brother about their relationship issues. This is crossing too many lines for her to count.

"I'd be happy to mention it to him the next time we're alone," Quinn offers.

"Quinn, I'm not sleeping. I'm not eating. I just have to know what's on his mind. He's off work today and has barely texted me. Is there any chance you could just stop by the house? Tell him you were on the way to see Heather."

Quinn has been meaning to stop by Heather's and check in on her. If Quinn is stressed over the media attention, she can't imagine how bad it's been for Heather.

"Fine. But, from now on, you two need to learn to communicate. We can't do this back and forth forever."

Jessie claps her hands together and then stands to hug Quinn, nearly leaping into her lap in the process.

"Why don't you respond to emails for another hour and maybe order Halloween costumes for Aiden and me? That will be your payment for me having to talk to my damn brother about his romantic relationships. I'll text you when I'm done, and we can meet somewhere to talk."

"I'll definitely get them ordered. What do you guys want to be? Romeo and Juliet? Superman and Superwoman?"

"I was thinking more along the lines of the wet bandits from Home Alone but pick whatever you'd like. Halloween has never really been my thing," Quinn responds. "I just want to be warm."

"All right, I got you," Jessie says with a wink.

Quinn doesn't even change out of her sweatpants to make the drive to Matt's house. She hasn't dreaded a meeting like this since the time her old agent wanted to meet up after her debut novel with the publisher wasn't performing as expected. It's not fun driving to a meeting when you know it's bad news. She regretted leaping from self-publishing the entire drive. When she was doing it alone, there were no disappointed agents or publishers, she could only disappoint herself.

Quinn knows Matt like the back of her hand, and if he's still acting strange with Jessie, it means he has cold feet. He's changed his mind. Just like Quinn knew would happen, which is why she cautioned Jessie against dating him. It will give her no pleasure to say *I told you so* in this situation.

She doesn't listen to a podcast for the drive, she simply cracks her windows and deeply inhales the crisp fall air. She also can't have the radio distracting her while she rehearses the speech she's going to give Matt about family functions going forward. If he thinks she's going to uninvite Jessie from holiday dinners just because he decided to break her heart, he's sadly mistaken.

She smiles when she pulls up to his house and can see the candles she bought him burning on the windowsill that faces the porch. So much for keeping the morbid décor only in the basement. The sun is just beginning to set, and between the flickering candles and the excessively ghoulish Halloween decorations in the front yard, it looks like a late October dream. Most days Quinn can't stand her brother, but they love each other in a way nobody will ever understand. She's so proud of him for buying this house on his own and not asking for her help, despite her protests.

She gives a few raps on the front door knocker, the oversized bronze skeleton one she purchased for him, and it vibrates the wooden door with each thwack. She can hear an old Halloween album playing on his record player. She rings the doorbell but doesn't hear any steps. Peeking through the window next to the door, she doesn't see him but knows he must be home because his vehicle is pulled up outside and the candles are lit. She steps back and calls his cell phone. She can hear it ringing inside. She pushes the door open slowly.

"Hey idiot, it's your sister!" she yells.

Nothing.

"Matt, you better not be naked!"

Nothing.

She moves through the entryway and into the living room. She instinctively leans forward to blow out his candles, remembering their mother's warning when they were young to never leave burning flames unattended.

Quinn now recognizes the song playing on the record player from the *Halloween Kills* soundtrack. Matt sang it for months after the movie came out.

Faces peeking out at us between the trees...Stop, look, and listen...It's Hall-o-ween

She pulls the needle off the record player and the house is silent.

"Matt!" she yells.

No response.

"This isn't funny. You're such an asshole. I know you're hiding."

She continues to walk through the kitchen, peeking into the guestroom and laundry room before gazing upstairs and deciding whether she has the patience to search another floor.

A quick, loud, clap sounds from the basement and startles Quinn so badly, she grabs the railing for support.

"Matt?"

She opens the basement door and can hear candles flickering gently, their flames bouncing off the otherwise dark room.

She slowly walks down the stairs and sees what appears to be a makeshift shrine at the bottom. Quinn remembers when Matt made a shrine to the devil in 9th grade because one of his death metal bands said it was the cool thing to do. Mom cried herself to sleep and Matt got grounded for a month.

As Quinn gets closer, she sees a small table with damaged cell phones next to the lit candles and small Ziploc bags scattered throughout. She leans forward and picks one up; there appears to be a lock of hair inside. There is a notecard in the center of the table, sitting on a copy of Quinn's book *Midnight,* and it looks to be written in Matt's shaky handwriting. There's only one line: I'm so sorry for this.

Panicked, Quinn reaches to her left and flips on the light switch for the basement.

She screams.

She briefly falls to her knees before regaining her balance and running forward.

J.L. Hyde

She sprints to the middle of the basement
where, from a thick metal pipe, her brother Matt is
hanging by a rope, swinging slowly, with a wooden
chair kicked over beneath him.

Chapter Thirty-Three

Quinn is fighting to keep her eyes open. She's been in this chair for three days without more than an hour of sleep at a time and it's beginning to show.

"Sweetheart, why don't you go home and take a nap? I promise I'll call you the minute he wakes up," her dad says, stroking her hair gently, and staring at his only son in the hospital bed before him.

Quinn completely ignores him and channels her rage at the policeman leaning on the door frame.

"Please, explain to me once more why one of his hands must be cuffed to the hospital bed. Do you think he's going to wake up and sprint out of here? This is inhumane."

The officer takes a deep breath and explains himself for the third time this afternoon.

"Mrs. Brooks, like I told you earlier, your brother is under arrest for the murder of three innocent people. I'm sorry you feel that one handcuff, loosely placed on his left wrist, is an inhumane treatment for a murder suspect."

"My brother didn't kill anyone; he wouldn't hurt a fly," Quinn speaks so low, it's nearly a growl.

"So you've told me," the officer says with a cocky grin. "That seems to be the reaction from every murder suspect's family, according to the shows on TV. You'd be surprised at the things we don't know about the private lives of our family members."

Jim slaps the table next to him, which makes them both jump. Quinn is nearly sure she saw Matt twitch at the loud noise.

"Hey Barney Fife, how about you stick to playing that dumb little game on your phone before I kick your ass so hard, they pick you up in El Paso for speeding."

The officer stands a little straighter and adjusts his belt.

"You can't threaten an officer of the law."

"It's not a threat, asshole, it's a promise."

The two men stare at each other for a long, uncomfortable thirty seconds, before the officer speaks again.

"I'm going to wait outside this room and give you three some privacy. It's obvious the trauma is affecting your judgment."

"Can't say you'll be missed," Jim responds.

"Bastard," the officer whispers under his breath before shutting the door.

Quinn looks up at her dad, who is still staring at the closed door. She can see the veins throbbing in his neck. She tries to focus on him, but her eyes are so heavy, they feel like weights have been glued to the lids. She'd give anything just for twenty or thirty minutes of rest, but she can't bear the thought of not being here when Matt wakes up. She can't wait to scream *I told you so* at the stupid cop as soon as her brother gives them a reasonable explanation for the evidence found in his basement.

Shortly after the officer leaves, there are two quick taps on the hospital room door before it swings open and the two homicide detectives, reportedly transferred up from Saginaw for the investigation, enter the room and approach Quinn and her dad.

"I was hoping we could catch you up on a few things the crime lab just sent over," the mustached, slightly overweight one says.

"Of course," Jim answers. Quinn knows he's eager to hear about this so-called evidence they think they have against his son.

"There were four cell phones found in the subject's basement."

Jim interrupts him.

"Matt. They were found in Matt's basement. He's not just the subject. He's my son, Matt."

The man blushes slightly and seems a bit flustered.

"The four cell phones in Matt's basement were all damaged, but we were able to trace three of them to the three victims in the strangling cases and the fourth is what we call a burner phone, loaded with prepaid minutes and untraceable."

Quinn inhales so sharply, all three heads turn to her. "You're sure they belonged to the victims?"

The second detective nods his head. "Yes ma'am, we are sure."

The first detective continues, reading from his notes as to avoid eye contact with Quinn and Jim.

"It appears texts and/or calls were placed to each victim shortly before their deaths from the burner phone, most likely to get the victims out of their homes and to a location of the suspect's…Matt's choosing. From what the crime lab was able to determine from the texts, he made the victims believe they were coming from persons known to them."

None of this makes sense. None of this seems like something Matt would be capable of. Sure, he's into gory horror films, but that doesn't mean he is capable of taking lives. He can barely handle responding to texts on his own phone (when he does respond, they are one-word answers) and these guys want Quinn to believe Matt purchased a burner phone and communicated well enough to gain the trust of three innocent people to lure them out of their homes and strangle them? No way. Also, everyone seems to think that the murderer modeled these crimes after one of her books. Quinn knows for certain that Matt doesn't even read her books; it's a fact he very proudly brings up each Thanksgiving after he's had a few spiked apple ciders. He says he does it to keep Quinn humble and every year, she rolls her eyes as the extended family laughs, assuming Matt is kidding.

"Please enlighten me as to what someone could have possibly said to Dottie Carlson to get that sweet woman out of her house past 8 pm. I've known her for years; she refused to drive in the dark at all unless it was an emergency."

Both detectives fidget slightly and look at each other, before turning their attention back to Quinn.

Mustache, who she now remembers is named Jacob, clears his throat.

"Quinn, I'm sorry to be the one to tell you this. Dottie left her house that night because she was under the impression she was meeting *you*."

Chapter Thirty-Four

When the doctor insists that Quinn saved her brother's life, she swears she detects a hint of resignation. Sure, she saved a life – but in his opinion, it's the life of someone who committed a triple homicide. She wonders if the doctor wishes she would have just let him hang.

The funny thing is she barely remembers any of it. She knows now that she grabbed a fishing knife out of his open tackle box (the same box that contained the rope during her last visit; the rope that somehow cannot be located now), flipped the wooden kitchen chair upright, lifted her 205lb brother with superhuman strength and cut him loose. She held him in her arms on the basement floor while she called 911 and sobbed, barely registering the CPR instructions the operator calmly recited. When the EMTs arrived and announced that they detected a faint heartbeat, Quinn leaned over and vomited in the tackle box.

Tonight is Devil's Night; the night before Halloween. What a bittersweet occasion — it's Matt's favorite holiday. Jessie briefly came up for air from her Xanax-induced nap to bring Matt's record player to the hospital with his favorite Halloween albums. She had to fight tooth and nail to be allowed in the house to retrieve them, as it's still considered a crime scene. Like Quinn and Jim, Jessie says it's just not possible that Matt could hurt anyone. The knowledge of Jessie and Quinn's conversation regarding Matt's strange behavior that morning gets buried deep; neither woman can bear to think of it now. There's just no way Matt did this.

As Jessie sets up the record player, Quinn is thankful, once again, that they aren't in a bigger city. There's no way they should be allowing visitors in the hospital room of a murder suspect, but the officers in Delta County most likely have never experienced anything like this and probably aren't quite sure how to handle it. She mentioned this in her book about Heather; the fact that Frank and Meryl were allowed in the room to watch her give birth while in custody would shock any family member of someone in the prison system. Small towns do things a little differently and it's not always with ill intent, it's often because they just haven't been in a situation like this before.

Heather texted Quinn this morning and asked if she could stop by in support of the family. Quinn wasn't sure if her arrival would create a bigger media firestorm than they were already experiencing, but she also didn't think it was possible to get any worse. The brother of famous author Quinn Harstead attempts to take his own life when authorities close in on him for being the Delta County Strangler. She hasn't opened her phone or laptop to see any of the headlines, but she imagines that's the gist.

Aiden has been going back and forth to the house to get food (this hospital stuff isn't cutting it, so Randall has been packaging up meals for the family) and clothes for Quinn, Jim, and Jessie. He doesn't feel comfortable trying to go to Matt and Jessie's house, so he's been grabbing extra outfits from Quinn's closet for her to wear. Just as he's leaving to go retrieve more supplies, Quinn receives a text that Heather is on her way. "Are you okay with that?" she asks Jessie.

"Makes no difference to me," Jessie says, void of emotion. Quinn notes from her glazed eyes that she must have taken another dose of anxiety meds. Quinn is in no place to judge. Her motto for grief is *whatever gets you through the day.*

Heather feels strange showing up at the hospital, but she knows it's the right thing to do. Quinn has been there for her more times than she can count since they met, and now it's time to repay the favor.

She had Meryl pick out a bouquet at Wickert Floral to bring for Quinn, but she wasn't sure what arrangement was best for the occasion of sympathizing with her friend because her only sibling is in a coma, while also being relieved that no one considers her a murder suspect anymore. Meryl settled on carnations.

It happened overnight. Heather received apologies from several members of the community who sheepishly admitted to doubting her innocence. Her friends' schedules suddenly cleared, and they immediately called or came over. Much to Meryl's delight, she was able to return to her beloved slot machines. The calls and emails from the media ceased briefly, before regaining their traction when they decided they needed Heather's thoughts on Quinn's brother seemingly framing her for murder.

Heather wasn't quite sure what to think about the situation. She has only met Matt a handful of times, and he acted indifferent at best toward her. She didn't sense a hint of animosity at any point. She didn't sense any feelings from him whatsoever. How could he possibly hate her enough to frame her for three murders? She has replayed the night she vented to Quinn about the roofer over and over in her mind. Quinn must have absentmindedly mentioned it to her brother, and he saw it as the perfect chance to once again murder someone connected to Heather. She also can't help but wonder what it was that finally did him in. Did he think he was about to get caught? Mitch mentioned that he felt the cops were close to nailing a suspect, and at the time, Heather just assumed he was saying that to make her feel better. Maybe they were on Matt's tail, and he sensed it, so he attempted to take his own life. If he survives, she cannot imagine how painful this trial is going to be if he doesn't plead guilty. How will Quinn manage to sit in a courtroom each day and hear these horrible things her brother did? Particularly to Dottie, whom Quinn loved dearly.

The sun is just beginning to set as Heather walks through the automatic doors of the hospital. She lifts the flowers slightly to obscure the sight of her face from anyone in the waiting room. Quinn has already told her what room they are in, so she bypasses the front desk and takes a right. She's relieved she doesn't have to turn left, which would have immediately triggered memories of the night her parents died. Thankfully, the hospital has done some remodeling in the last decade or so, which makes it slightly less triggering for her. The hallways are decorated with black construction paper cutouts in the shape of bats and pumpkins carved with toothless grins. There are also Get Well Soon cards taped throughout the hall, and she smiles as she leans forward to see that they were drawn by elementary students from the local Catholic school.

She knows room 313 is on the corner, not because she knows the layout of the hospital, but because she can see an armed guard sitting outside. He stands as she approaches and she recognizes him as a boy, or man now, that she went to school with.

"Heather Green, good to see you out and about."

"Hey Billy, it's good to be out and about," she replies with a smile.

"Well, we've actually got this asshole to thank," he whispers, pointing his thumb toward the closed hospital door. "Maybe we can all get back to normal lives now that he's been caught."

She gives him a slight, uncomfortable smile.

"Sorry to say, I'm actually here to visit that asshole."

He looks like he's been slapped. Surprise turned to anger. His whisper is now loud enough to border on full volume. "You do know this man murdered three innocent people, and from what I hear, tried to pin it on you, right Heath?"

"It's a long, complicated story, Billy."

"Well, I can't let you in any way. Sarge says family only."

She's not in the mood to argue with him. Or anyone, for that matter.

"Understandable. Would you mind just peeking your head in and telling Quinn I'm here? Maybe she can come out so I can say hello and give her these flowers I bought."

He appears to consider it for a moment and apparently can't think of a good enough excuse to refuse her request. He furrows his brow and nods before slowly opening the door, entering, and closing it behind him. After a minute or two, he reopens the door and has the unmistakable look of someone who was just berated by Jim Harstead.

"You can go in for a minute, but please make it quick. I'm not trying to lose my job."

"Of course, Billy, I'll be in and out," Heather says, patting his arm as she passes him in the doorway.

Heather hugs Quinn and Jim, before awkwardly greeting Jessie. They don't quite know each other well enough for an embrace, but Heather doesn't want to appear cold or thoughtless. It also occurs to her in this moment that she should have brought two bouquets, but it's too late for that now.

"For the room, I hope it brightens it up a bit," Heather says, trying to save the situation.

"That's incredibly kind of you," Jessie says, accepting the flowers and placing them on a table by the window.

"What's the latest?" Heather asks, turning her gaze to Matt. Aside from his bloated face and bruised neck, he appears to be sleeping. If it weren't for the beeping machines and tubes everywhere, she'd never know he was in a coma. She stares hard at him and tries to figure out if she's looking at the face of a murderer. She hasn't been filled in on the evidence they found in Matt's basement, but one of the officers who came to her house referred to it as "incredibly incriminating." Could this be the man who murdered her beloved Dottie, a woman his sister also loved?

"They said it's a waiting game. They did an MRI of his brain that shows evidence of what they call an anoxic injury. Even if he does wake up, there's no telling the amount of brain damage he could have from the period that he was cut off from oxygen. Step one is him waking up, step two would be assessing the damage. Right now, we are just praying for him to wake up," Quinn tells her.

Heather continues to stare at Matt, lying in the bed with one wrist in a handcuff. She thinks of how silly it is for these officers to handcuff him to the bed; do they honestly think he could just wake up and run off?

As she focuses on his face, she swears she sees his eyelids twitch. Quinn sees it, too, and explains, "They tell us those twitches are involuntary and nothing we should be overly excited about."

Matt's entire body stirs and Heather turns to Quinn to see if this also qualifies as involuntary. Quinn seems surprised to see his body moving. One of the machines begins beeping at a quicker pace and everyone in the room stares at the man lying in the bed before them. His eyes begin to flutter at a rapid speed, before opening wide. He looks panicked, his head and eyes darting in every direction, before looking down at the tubes coming out of his arms and the cuff on his left wrist. He opens his mouth to speak, but nothing comes out. His eyes focus on Heather, and he begins slapping the bed wildly with his free hand, before lifting it and pointing his index finger directly at her. Every head in the room turns to her in horror.

"Me?" she gasps, her hand over her heart.

"You?" Jessie asks slowly, with a delirious look in her eyes. "You," she repeats.

Chapter Thirty-Five

Jessie lunges toward Heather, but Jim and Quinn both leap in front of her to stop the attack.

"I didn't do anything!" Heather yells.

Everyone turns to Matt as he slaps the table next to him to get their attention. He's shaking his head no and motioning for Jessie to get away from Heather. His hand moves to his throat, and he flinches in pain when he touches the bruised and swollen skin.

They rush to his bedside as Quinn turns to Heather and shouts, "Get a doctor! Tell them he's awake!"

Heather, slightly in shock, pulls open the door and sprints out of the room, turning back to Billy to shout where she's going. She makes it to the nurse's station, words barely forming as she struggles to catch her breath.

"We need help, Matt Harstead's awake!"

The next few moments are a blur for everyone involved. The family is ushered out of the room and the door is closed behind them. Officer Billy remains at the door, on guard as instructed. His eyes are filled with panic and it's clear that he never expected Matt to wake up. He thought his job was going to be mindless; he was guarding a man in a coma.

Jim and the three women pace the halls, ignoring the dozens of empty chairs they could sit in while they wait for the doctor. Heather catches each of them looking at her out of the corner of her eye, and according to her Apple Watch, her heart rate is at 138 bpm. She knows Matt was simply confused when he woke up. Obviously, he didn't mean to point at her. This will all be cleared up in a minute when they can see him again. She will gladly and kindly accept an apology from Jessie for trying to attack her. She's sure she would do the same thing in her shoes. In fact, she has.

They hear the squeak of dress shoes turning the corner and picking up pace as they sprint down the hallway. It's the two detectives, who were contacted by Billy with the news as soon as Matt woke up. They seem relieved to see everyone still in the hallway. Both men stop to catch their breath when they reach the door.

"As soon as the doctors are done and give us the okay, we will be in to question him. Alone."

Jim begins to argue, before Jacob, the detective, holds up his hand. "Mr. Harstead, your son is technically in our custody. You are all incredibly fortunate that you've been allowed to be at his bedside since he got here, something I argued against from the get-go. I'm going to draw the line here."

For once in his life, Jim Harstead simply nods in agreement and hangs his head. The hospital door opens slightly and the doctor on duty waves the detectives inside. He speaks to them for a moment before he and two nurses exit the room and close the door behind them.

"What I can tell you is that Matt's vitals are currently stable. He is awake and alert but doesn't currently have a voice, most likely due to the damage done to his vocal cords by the rope used in the incident, rather than from the lack of oxygen. It's going to be a waiting game before we can assess the total damage, particularly to his brain. His blood tests upon admission showed some pretty extreme levels of doxylamine from sleeping pills he ingested before attempting to take his life."

The door to Matt's room opens before anyone can ask any follow-up questions. Jacob peeks his head out and asks for a dry-erase board. One of the nurses nods, pulls one off the wall behind her and hands it to Jacob. He again closes the door.

"So, you're telling me we aren't even sure if my son has brain damage, but we're allowing him to be questioned by the police?" Jim asks.

"Do you want me to call Doug Angeli?" Heather asks.

Before either man can answer the questions posed, the door again swings open and both detectives come running out. "Come on, Billy!" Jacob yells. After a beat, Billy sprints after them.

Everyone, including the nurses and doctor, are stunned. Quinn and Jessie run into Matt's room and straight to his bedside. He is crying. They hug him as gently as they can without disturbing any of the lines hooked to his body and begin to cry, too.

Jim slowly walks in behind them. "What in the hell was that about?"

Matt wipes his face and points to his bedside table, where the dry-erase board has been thrown, face down. Quinn turns it around and she and Jessie read it, before looking up at Heather.

There are obvious signs of haphazardly erased answers that were drawn over as the detectives asked rapid-fire questions to Matt.

There's only one word left on the board, written in capital letters, and underlined three times.

RYAN

Part Four: Ryan

Chapter Thirty-Six

He knows he should be upstairs helping Julie get ready for the holiday tomorrow, but he can't bring himself to stop obsessing over the news of Matt's arrest and current condition. He keeps refreshing the news pages on his laptop, waiting for an update. He has even gone as far as sending a nonchalant text to Heather, asking if she's heard anything. This was supposed to be simple. He should be dead. Just like the rest.

When Heather mentioned she wanted to go visit him in the hospital, Ryan was surprised, but he immediately volunteered to come to get Evie. This was the surest way to get Heather to the hospital quickly so she could give him the inside scoop on Matt's condition.

He cannot believe the bastard survived. It would have been a perfect crime, had Quinn not come over and ruined everything. His plan was for the sleeping pills to kick in so Matt wouldn't fight back as Ryan fastened the noose. Instead, he had to hold a gun to his head and threaten to kill him and Quinn both if he responded to her voice, which sounded like it was getting closer and closer to the basement stairs. He panicked and had no choice but to strangle him with the rope before hanging him from the ceiling, which was no easy feat. He was certain he didn't feel a pulse but couldn't wait to find out as he heard Quinn's footsteps. He kicked the chair out from underneath Matt and scrambled back out the basement window where he originally entered. He was back in the car before he realized he still had the rest of the rope in the front pocket of his hoodie, along with the engagement ring he found Matt sitting on the couch and staring at when he caught him by surprise an hour earlier. He still can't believe Matt was planning on proposing to that mousy little blonde that's always tagging along with Quinn Harstead. What could he possibly see in her?

Speaking of Quinn Harstead, the original plan was obviously to frame her. The stupid, careless woman who painted him as an adulterous asshole in a book that was read by millions. He received so much hate mail, he quit opening the envelopes at all. His mother was already gone, and she tried to kill his reputation, too. He should have finished her stupid little novel to see that the main character was the killer, not some faceless man. He never meant to make the community point their fingers at Heather, but once the narrative fit, he had to kill that roofer to keep the pattern going. This all seemed like a good idea until he realized the mother of his youngest child would be spending the rest of her life in prison and having another infant around full-time wouldn't exactly suit his lifestyle. He needed to pin it on someone else. He didn't have any particular animosity toward Matt Harstead, he was just the perfect person to frame. It made sense.

Now he sits in his basement, staring at the box of mementos from each of his murders. Mementos he never meant to keep, but now he's glad he did. He hates that he had to get rid of their cell phones, but knew they were needed to properly frame Matt and assure there were no loose ends. Now Quinn can suffer as she should. Her brother is a killer and took his own life in shame. Her writing inspired his crimes. If all goes as planned, she may never write another book for as long as she lives.

Ryan keeps opening his phone to check for a text from Heather, confirming Matt has died. Or, even better, Matt lives but he's a vegetable that can't think or talk. That would give Quinn Harstead sufficient suffering.

Ryan continues fidgeting with the engagement ring meant for Matt's girlfriend. It's small and sad and Ryan knows Matt probably should have asked his sister for money so he could buy a proper ring. What a pathetic man.

Ryan hears a commotion upstairs and assumes Julie has invited over a few of her insufferable friends. That idea changes when he hears male voices. He stands in confusion as the basement door flies open and a fleet of officers storm the room.

"Ryan Matthews, you are under arrest for the murders of Susan Grant, Dottie Carlson, Kent Savard, and the attempted murder of Matthew

Harstead," one of the officers shouts, body slamming Ryan on the ground and handcuffing him behind his back.

As he is led up the stairs, he passes Julie, who is holding a crying Evie and grasping Hunter's tiny toddler hand.

"Call my dad," he says calmly, and she nods.

"Ma'am, you're going to have to take the kids and find somewhere to stay for the next day or two while we search the house."

"Of course, officer," she responds, wiping a tear from her cheek and shushing Evie as she bounces her on her hip.

As the officers leave, she watches them load Ryan in the back of the police car. He makes eye contact with her and gives her a brief wink. She nods in response. She takes out her phone to shoot Heather a quick text; she's going to need to drop Evie off, and she'll explain when she gets there.

Julie then walks upstairs to their massive master bedroom and pulls a packed duffle bag from beneath the California King-sized bed they share. She smiles to herself as she considers how much better they've gotten at preparation since college when they were young, inexperienced, and made reckless mistakes. She knew she'd have to pack for a night or two away if either of them made a mistake big enough to get caught. Lucky for her, it was Ryan who got caught first.

Epilogue

NINE MONTHS LATER

"Oh my god, Heather!"

Heather sprints up the stairs and dashes into Evie's room. Mitch and Evie are sitting on the rug in the center of the room, playing with her dolls. Mitch is wearing a pink boa around his neck and has a child's size plastic princess tiara on his head.

"What? What happened?" she gasps.

Mitch smiles.

"Oh, we just wanted to remind you that we love you."

Heather throws her head back in frustration and lifts two fingers to her neck to feel her racing pulse. "You have got to stop doing that!"

Evie laughs furiously and claps her hands. It's her favorite prank. *Scare Mommy.* Her beautiful, perfect, angelic laugh is all Heather needs to forgive Mitch for his nonsense. She walks over to him, removes his tiara, and puts it on her head. He stands in retaliation and wraps his arms around her, blowing raspberries on her neck as she laughs uncontrollably. Evie continues to clap and scream with laughter.

"Okay, okay, I love you guys, too!" Heather screams, begging Mitch to stop tickling her neck with his lips. "I have told you that I hate being tickled, Mitch Miller."

"And I have told you that nothing makes me happier than hearing you girls laugh, so I guess I win this argument."

Heather rolls her eyes and kisses Mitch on the cheek and leans over to do the same to the top of Evie's head.

"Okay, I just need you guys to stay up here and be quiet for the next twenty minutes. Fair?" Heather asks.

Mitch looks at Evie and asks her if she agrees. She nods and holds her index finger up to her tiny pink lips. Mitch does the same and smiles.

"Thank you, my loves, I'll let you know the minute I'm done."

Heather dashes across the hall to check her appearance in the master bathroom. She begins to obsess over the zit forming on her chin and the crease in her hair from her ponytail this morning, but she decides to ignore them both. She's doing this. There's no going back.

She pads down the stairs and retrieves her phone from the kitchen counter. She responds to a text from Quinn about their plans to go shopping in Green Bay this weekend and a text from Meryl about dinner at her and Frank's house tomorrow. She smiles when she glances at today's mail, which Mitch has thrown on the island. The latest issue of People

Magazine is lying face-up, with Matt Harstead on the cover. He's sitting on the front steps of the rehabilitation center he just moved out of, with the word **Survivor** written underneath. Quinn, Jessie, and Jim are sitting on the steps behind him. Jessie has a beautiful diamond engagement ring on her left hand.

She nearly changes her mind for the millionth time before walking into the living room and sitting on the couch. She takes a deep breath, opens the Instagram app, and clicks "reactivate account." She tries to ignore the rapid beating of her heart as she snaps the phone into her tripod, which is set up on the coffee table in front of her. She clicks a small plus symbol in the top right corner and then selects "live" from the drop-down list.

She smiles, fidgets with her hair for a moment, and exhales.

"Hi everyone. It's Heather, live on Ogden Avenue. It's been a while, and boy, do I have a lot to catch you guys up on, so buckle in. I've missed you."

J.L. Hyde

Acknowledgments

Each time I finish another book, the list of people I get to thank increases. I can't tell you how good that feels.

First and foremost, my proofreaders/beta-readers/whatever you'd like to call them. I have a handful of people whom I trust to give me honest advice when I finish a book and each of them brings something different to the table.

Cash, you're always the last to finish reading but have the most notes and I love you for that, even when I act as if it aggravates me.

Ruth, your knowledge of format, grammar, word usage, etc. is second to none. You are no-nonsense and never sugarcoat your feedback. I appreciate you more than you know.

Kim, you're my big sister and biggest fan but have no problem telling me when something's not working, and I love you for that.

John, you are the best combination of being my personal hype-man, while also being brutally honest, which is just what I need.

April, you started as a reader and became a friend. I can't think of a better person to give me feedback.

Marissa, I don't know how you found the time to read this book with a newborn, but I can't thank you enough. Also, thank you for letting me borrow her name for this book. I promise to donate to her college fund as often as I can for the trouble, hah!

I have someone new to thank for this novel and her name is Stephanie, but you may know her on TikTok as @sellingnwa. She was once my favorite account to get suggestions on new books to read but became even more to me when she stumbled upon my books and changed everything. Because of Stephanie, my books got in front of thousands of readers and then picked up by dozens of other reviewers. Stephanie, you changed my life and I'm so lucky to now call you a friend.

To all the accounts that review books on Instagram, Facebook, TikTok, and Twitter: You have no idea how much you've changed my entire situation. I will never stop thanking you. Your words and enthusiasm for my writing mean more than you know.

To my best friends who constantly support me, make me laugh, encourage me to keep writing, and celebrate successes with me: I love you and don't know what I'd do without you. Specifically, Mal, who is my unofficial and unpaid spokeswoman.

To Samantha Kersten: You are the first person to ever leave me a book review online and I'll never forget how good it felt to read it. Although I haven't had the pleasure of meeting you in real life yet, your support has meant so much. Thank you for letting me borrow your husband for the sake of this book. I know I made him seem a little worse than he is, but I didn't kill him off so that's something, right? Thank you, Matt, for being a good sport and always sending me the best horror movie recommendations.

Alena: You are my friend first and my audiobook narrator second, but I'm equally grateful for both roles you play in my life. I can't wait to see what the future holds.

To Brandon and Ty at Allsweet Studios: I have never met two men so kind, generous, talented, and enthusiastically on board to help a girl you haven't even known that long. I'll spend the rest of my days trying to repay you for your services and friendship.

To Kevin, Jason, and the rest of the team at Visit Escanaba: I will never stop promoting our great little town. Thank you both for saving me in the 11th hour.

To my Delta County ladies: I'm counting down the minutes until I'm home and can repay you for all you continue to do for me. The Toilet Paper Vixens shall ride again.

Lindsey, thank you for being my resident medical expert and never (or rarely) judging me for my silly questions.

To my family, thank you for the support you continue to show. I know we all wish Mom and Dad were here to join in the celebration, but I know they are somewhere smiling.

Jack and Alec, thank you for going to bat for a girl you barely know. I'm looking forward to seeing what kind of magic we can make out of a little book set in northern Michigan.

To the readers: You're the most important part of it all. There just are no words to describe how it feels when you enjoy one of my books and spread the word to your loved ones. Word of mouth and reviews are what keep me in business, and I'll never take them for granted. Thank you for always reminding me that there are a lot more kind and decent people in this world than bad.

If you enjoyed this book, clicking 5 stars on Amazon, Audible, GoodReads, or wherever you review books helps me more than you could imagine.

If you'd like to reach out or follow me on social media:

Email: info@JLHyde.com
Facebook: Author JL Hyde
Instagram: @bookandbeerreview
TikTok: @authorJLHyde
Website: www.JLHyde.com

www.ingramcontent.com/pod-product-compliance
Lightning Source LLC
Chambersburg PA
CBHW020337180726
47991CB00020B/1731